DAYS WHEN THE HOUSE WAS TOO SMALL

DAYS
WHEN THE HOUSE
WAS TOO SMALL

DYCKMAN ANDRUS

Charles Scribner's Sons
New York

Library of Congress Cataloging in Publication Data
Andrus, Dyckman.
    Days when the house was too small.
    I. Title.
PZ4.A574Day [PS3551.N456]   813′.54   74-8079
ISBN 0-684-13898-0

1 3 5 7 9 11 13 15 17 19 c/c 20 18 16 14 12 10 8 6 4 2

Printed in the United States of America

For Robert Model with Thanks

CONTENTS

DAYS WHEN THE HOUSE WAS TOO SMALL

DAYS WHEN THE HOUSE
WAS TOO SMALL

One | There had been a sunrise raging red across the lake through the pines to the caretaker's cabin. Now the sky had lost color and the snow was stiff and old. It was still early morning.

Fred Macken sat in the kitchen at the table with his wife Hilda. Fred was moody and Hilda was fingering the sunflower seeds. They were looking out at everything they could see. They saw nothing they didn't know and none of it helped them.

"Where's Mory?" Fred asked.

"In his room reading."

"He's always reading. How come he reads so much?"

"He don't have nothing else to do," the woman said. "That sky don't look so good."

"I seen it like this before. You can't tell what it's going to do."

"Well, it won't rain."

"When's it going to end?" the caretaker asked the window.

"I can't tell, Fred."

"I wish I could do something. I feel like a shut-in sitting around here all the time."

"We'll be doing something when we get ready for the party."

"That ain't what I mean, Ma. Where's them kids?"

"Still sleeping. They was tired."

"They're always tired."

"We could go for a ride."

"Where to?"

"I don't know. Do you want something to eat, Pa?"

"I couldn't eat. I woke up feeling so good. The sun was shining. I felt so good I was going to fix that truck."

"I felt much better, too. My arms wasn't so sore."

The caretaker stifled a burp and said, "It's getting to look like spring won't ever come."

"The calendar says it's coming."

"That ain't what I mean. The calendar says it's George Washington's birthday when it ain't."

"He's dead so it don't matter."

"That's right, Ma. Dead don't matter. You know something? What I can't understand is now they want to let that kid throw out the first baseball. I mean, who is he anyway? Always before if the president or the vice-president couldn't do it, they'd at least go get a statesman to fill in. Like one of them off the Supreme Court. Now they let a kid do it and it ain't right. I'm sick of looking at that kid."

"His grandfather was the president," Hilda said.

"Well he ain't no more and, like you just said, dead don't matter."

Hilda put the seeds back in the saucer. They sounded like pebbles.

"Did you hear on the radio what they said in one of them books? Not the *Daily News*, but one of them other books down in New York City?"

"What'd they say, Ma?"

"I don't know if I can get it right. I heard it last night on one of the stations. You were sleeping. It wasn't CBS. I couldn't get that too good."

"For Christsake, Hilda, what was it?"

"About how with the kid doing everything, flying around in them special planes, he was becoming a monarchy."

"It sure looks like it. Who's he think he is?"

"They say it's worse than them Kennedys were."

"They wasn't so bad now."

"I don't know about all of them but I can still feel sorry for the women."

"Yeah, if I live long enough one of them girls who was at that party where they went off the bridge is going to spill it all."

"I can't say that bridge name right yet."

"Them girls can't resist that kind of money. That's what I'm waiting for."

"I'd like that," Hilda said. "That'll be good."

"You know it's been eight months today, Ma."

"For what, dear?" She sat up for the answer.

Fred looked over at the shotgun in the corner near the door. It was an old twelve gauge with a single rusty barrel and an outside hammer. The stock was scratched and held together with black electrician's tape where it was cracked. It was a close-range weapon and Fred kept it loaded. It wasn't meant for intruders or to kill anything more than blue jays although it could. Fred used it for the birds. He hated blue jays as much as he hated anything.

"Since I quit smoking," the caretaker said and he began unzipping his coveralls.

"The roads is probably bad," Hilda said. "I hope it don't snow no more."

They were both looking out the window. It was still early and it was such a gray morning.

Two | Fall that year was first glances of strong color on the Adirondack peaks across the lake. And later others, lingering, at darkest ruffles of the long lake stirred by northern winds before freezing black. Then fall was very gone with Christmas behind quietly. Wool scarves were worn again, wrapped tightly at dry throats while the tough people wearing them hurried and refused to sneeze. Then there were the long winter nights and shrunken days when Mory Keller never left the brown house near the broken twisted highway. There was nothing for the boy outside. Always it was cold.

In January the plastic thermometer outside the bay window stayed stuck near zero. The instrument was the Christmas gift of an Indian charity through the mails, a fragile bit of thin red tube ending in a lost bulb. The boy's stepfather had fixed it permanently with a rusty tack and Mory consulted it daily and treated it with respect, like a bobcat hide or an almost precious relic. But the thermometer was Fred's job.

And in January the back door to the kitchen warped open so the caretaker had to fix it, first with a chair, later off its hinges with a plane, a blanket tacked temporarily across the door. Then the drainpipe beneath the kitchen sink snapped and for three days Mory's mother cleaned her dishes in two plastic tubs set in the sink and threw the wash and rinse waters onto the driveway where they froze gray. Fred fixed the pipe too, finally.

Always the boy Mory sat stonily in the frayed green corner lounger by the bay window where he could read the sky or watch the sets of skis sliding by on car roofs beyond the snowbank of the plowed highway. The fresh snow would rise softly behind the cars and their exhausts would billow over the bank like warm white spray. When there was a breath of wind from the sleeping hill across the road, the fumes would push against the window at Mory like a rich rolling ground fog he was forbidden to smell. After, the road would be settled again and quiet and the sky left to admire. Maybe there would be another loaded logging truck bound for Tupper Lake and south to the pulp mills. The boy would hear the heavy tires squeak the ice beneath the snow and see the plaid-jacket drivers hunch their wheels and use the whole road where they could. But mostly there were skiers in January.

Then in February came a chinook and for one week the skiers stayed home. A cold rain drenched the snow into dark sinking wells beneath the naked branches of the trees on the hill and twigs and bits of broken branches appeared on the snow and the monster road plows could stay safely in their green State sheds. Then Mory could have gone outside except he didn't.

And then it was arctic cold again and windy and if it did not snow at night it snowed in the morning or later that evening. But less now, like a little. The storms were called snowshowers on the radio in late February, as if they were warmer. The thermometer came unstuck and the bobsled run near Lake Placid closed but the skiing was better than ever everywhere.

Mory Keller was badly burned in August. The boy had been painting the camp lodge with his stepfather. There were no guests. Samuel Weaver who owned the camp for his own pleasure and a few select summer guests had not been there. He had been touring Europe with his wife and two sons. The Weavers had returned for Labor Day when Mory was still in the hospital and Weaver and his wife had come to see him. Weaver had paid the doctor bills and Mrs. Weaver had said she was sorry.

The accident was stupid. Fred was painting the walls above a window and using an aluminum stepladder which was unsteady. He was smoking and complaining both about the ladder and how Samuel Weaver never carried compensation insurance for his employees as the other camp owners on the lake did. Mory was working underneath when Fred's cigarette dropped into the paint thinner and exploded the can. The ignited liquid grabbed Mory like white phosphorous, burning off his lightweight clothes completely before Fred made him roll in the sandy driveway. Everything had hurt at once and Mory had known clearly everything happening to him but he was too scared to scream above his own burning smell. The old comfortable lodge did not catch fire but some of the unraked pine needles on the ground near the window were burning loosely when Fred backed the station wagon up to the boy to take him to the hospital. His mother had helped wrap him in a blanket and load him and Fred had called her Hilda instead of Ma when he ordered her to alert the hospital they were coming. She was crying when they left her to watch for any new fires.

Mory's burns were packed with sand and the can shrapnel had left holes in his skin. The wounds covered most of his back and legs and part of his stomach and chest. They missed his face except around his eyes. But he was a strong boy and by Thanksgiving he was standing up under his wounds and moving around in his soft new skin with only occasional pain to remind him he was lucky. His hair came back quickly but his seeing was troubled because of possible retina damage when he fell. It wasn't serious enough to require immediate exploration or surgery.

After the accident Fred had not smoked again. He had sworn to quit at the emergency room. After he got home he had posted a sign on the kitchen door that warned that smoking was prohibited inside the house. He didn't want to be reminded of the smell of tobacco and the sign reminded everyone who came by how Fred had quit smoking.

Now early in March Mory had lost a year of school and he still could not work or move quickly without some annoyance. Each day he dressed himself in antiseptic white as though white clothing were a required uniform for the once burned. Except for the occasional pair of khaki trousers, his clothes were completely white and his mother had knitted him a white sweater for Christmas.

Three | The lounge chair in the corner of the living room was the best place for Mory. He could watch both the road and the television and hear any conversation in the kitchen or when it was very quiet, in the rest of the small brown caretaker's house. Mory was seventeen and he needed to know everything. With little effort he could lean the chair back and lay on his back and have the leg rest come up under his feet comfortably. Or he could sit up perfectly straight like an astronaut in his command module. There were also a variety of nice positions in between.

The lounge chair had been Fred's but now it was Mory's, like a reparation, and now his stepfather sat on the sofa in another corner. The caretaker's new space was directly opposite the television which was a wide screen color set from Montgomery Ward.

When the change of seats became permanent, Fred moved a tin tray with folding metal legs in front of his new place. The table was always covered with crossword puzzles torn from newspapers and the dictionaries needed to help solve them. They were only swept aside to eat. Then they were replaced. Actually the scant metal table had replaced a larger coffee table which serviced the entire couch because Fred had discovered he developed heartburn from bending over to eat dinner off the lower table while watching television. The tray contraption gave him less room to work his puzzles but it was suitably higher.

Mory heard his stepfather click his full set of dentures

as he thumbed one of the dog-eared dictionaries. Fred whistled tunelessly through the false teeth and then he was quiet for a long minute before he spoke.

"I need a five-letter word for flower, Ma," the caretaker said gradually. "I know it but I just can't think of it."

"Pansy," Hilda said and she smiled. She was sitting in her special chair, a low rocker which made her body bunch up and look like an old soft potato. She wasn't rocking. She wasn't doing anything but sitting and staring at the blank screen of the television.

"That's good, Ma, but it don't fit."

"But ain't it five letters?"

"Yeah, Hilda, it's five letters but it's got to have 'c' on the end."

"You didn't say that. Why do they make them puzzles so hard?"

"It ain't hard," Fred said. He was always slightly disgusted with her simplicity when he was working puzzles. "It's just that I can't think. I don't know why I can't think."

"You're tired, dear. That's why. And you may have caught a little cold when you was trying to fix that truck. You shouldn't have stayed out so long."

"What could I do?" Fred asked, closing the dictionary. "I had to get it fixed. That damn truck. I don't know why he wants to keep that truck. What good is it? He's ruined everything on it. I got to spend five hours every time fixing it for one hour of plowing."

"The boss sure likes it though," Mory said. He remembered how often Samuel Weaver had told him that the Dodge Power Wagon was the best vehicle he owned. He owned a lot of them. The first move Weaver made when he got to camp was to start the truck.

"Yeah, well why don't he think of me once in awhile?" Fred said. "I'm the one who's always got to fix it. He just don't understand things wear out. Like them vacuum cleaners he makes Ma use. He thinks once you buy something it's going to last forever and be perfect. I don't care what it is. And he thinks I ruin everything. Like that outboard motor. Me. That truck wasn't no good to start with. I told him but he wouldn't listen. He don't need that much power. He just don't listen to nothing I say no more. That old truck we had was better than this one. All's it needed was a new rear end."

Fred sat back. He took off his glasses to rub his eyes. They were both red. Out of the coveralls in the warm house he was wearing a T-shirt and his once powerful arms shook when he moved them. The muscles seemed to be rearranging themselves under the pale, wrinkled skin. His fly had worked open where his belt bunched his trousers and he caught the zipper with his free hand. Fred's hair was gray and quite long where he combed it over the bald spot in back. For a working man he looked very clean.

"Mr. Weaver wanted a whole new truck," Mory said comfortably.

"Yeah, why?" Fred asked. His voice was froggy and he replaced his glasses. "I'll tell you why. It was after he went to Idaho hunting that moose or whatever it was. Remember? Some know-it-all told him Dodges was better than Ford or Chevy. So he had to have a Dodge. A Power Wagon that could climb Pike's Peak. What do them cowboys know out there. They got snow like this here?"

"I know they got snow," Hilda said. She was smiling but she was never pretty when she smiled because her front teeth were bad. She was ten years younger than Fred. He was her third husband and he liked her to try to look pretty because it made him feel younger. But in the winter when they rarely went anywhere Hilda never wore makeup and gave little attention to her dark brown hair. Her hair was the prettiest part of her. Mostly in the winter she wore baggy linted sweaters, old skirts or ski pants, scuffed fleece-lined boots, and her red-framed spectacles. She was never a pretty woman when it was cold.

"You see them on the TV sometimes," Hilda said. "Trying to feed their cows with them heliocopters."

"Helicopters, Ma," Fred said. "But like this? With this cold? Constantly?"

"I don't know," the woman said. "I think I seen them."

"It does look like this," Mory said to help her. He was sitting way back.

"Yeah, well, you can't never believe what you see on television no more. Agnew told us that. Anyhow I bet they got heated garages to fix their plows in Montana. Them rich ranchers. I bet they don't got to freeze their ass off like I do. I bet they got trucks that work, too. And, look here, what do they know about Montana in New York City where they make them shows anyway?"

"It was Idaho, Fred, where Mr. Weaver went. Or Iowa."

"Same thing," the caretaker said.

Mory said slowly, "Someday I'd like to see Idaho."

"What for?"

"The fish."

"Be grateful for what you got," Fred said. "Someday I'd like to see the boss do his own plowing."

"Tulip," Hilda said suddenly. She was all smiles.

"Does that end with a 'c'?" Fred asked. He had resumed his finger patrol of the dictionary. "I told you it had to end in 'c'. Besides it's got to be a Whitman poetry."

"You didn't say that."

"Would it have helped?"

"Pa," Hilda said, "you always make me feel so stupid." The woman folded her hands in her lap and stared at the dark screen. It was as though she were finished trying to help and would now concentrate on television things which were not there.

"You're not so stupid, Ma. You just act that way."

"Oh, Fred," Hilda said but she was smiling.

"Come on, Mory. You're the bright one. You're supposed to know poets. What did they teach you in school about Mr. Whitman?"

Mory was leaning as far back as he could. His legs were all the way up so his white socks and sneakers hung out over the leg rest. He was looking sideways out the window when he said, "Lilacs."

"It ain't supposed to be a plural so that could be it," Fred said. He was sitting up straight and leaning over the puzzle. They heard him pick up the stubby wooden pencil to write in the word.

"Now why didn't I think of that?"

"Lilacs," Hilda said. "Good, Mory. Where did you know about Whitening and them poets?"

Mory looked sadly at his mother.

"Here comes Martin," he said.

Four | Martin Findle was caretaker to the next camp. He didn't live on the upper lake all year. He owned a house in town and during the winter he drove out to check his camp. He was the same old age as Fred but he acted younger and was well organized. When he couldn't do something necessary, he didn't complain or not do it. He hired someone who could.

For ten years Martin had driven the same old car with the same loose muffler and floorboards. Even in winter he kept the car windows down, and then he wore too much clothing to counter the cold.

When they heard him stomp the mat, Fred said, "I wonder what in hell he wants."

He rose to open the door.

"Hello, old boy," Martin said. He never changed. He was shy and serious but friendly.

"What you doing out this way, old boy?" Fred asked. "Come on in."

"What you up to, old boy?"

"Nothing," said Fred.

"That's about what I figured," said Martin.

"Care to come in, old boy, or you want to stand out there insulting me? You're freezing the guts out of my house."

Briefly both men laughed.

"Can only stay a minute, Fred."

"Could you stand a shot?"

"No thanks. I see you had your dinner."

"I didn't eat much. Didn't feel hungry. I don't know what's wrong with me today. Ma's going to fix a big supper of ribs."

"You ain't been poaching?"

"We're having a party after."

"I heard."

"Where'd you hear, old boy?"

"Jack was in town." Jack was Martin's only son.

"Ain't he got a big mouth?"

"He don't say much."

"If you want, come on out later. We didn't think Eva would care to come or we'd have called you." Martin's wife was Eva.

"She couldn't make it now, Fred."

"How's she doing, old boy?"

"Poor, Fred. Those pills she's been taking lately don't seem to help. I've had the worst part of a cold myself."

"Shit, you look good," Fred said. Then like a child with a newly learned rhyme he said, "Martin looks good. Yes he does. He sure looks good. Better than I feel."

"You sick too?"

"With what I got to do around here there's no way I can feel anything but sick."

"With me it's my damn lungs," Martin said. "That's what the doctor told me. I can only go so long. Then I got to stop. I just came out to check my ice machine. Almost didn't make it through that snow at the boathouse. Must be five feet of it down at the dock."

"I'd have gone over to check it for you but Ma's been sick again. She didn't have a good night."

"Lucky I came though," Martin said.

"How's that, old boy? You sure you won't have a shot? Fix you up in no time."

"You know that compressor I got? Well, you know how big that intake is? You could run a hurricane through it. When I got down there this morning, it looked like a bird's been nesting in it. I don't know where all that stuff come from. Them pipes wasn't getting no air."

"Told you you should have bought one like mine. I ain't had no ice trouble in three years. It works good."

"Mine's good, Fred. Only I did make them holes a little too big."

"Froze up on you did it? You better come all the way in, Martie. Or we'll both freeze."

"It's all right now," Martin said.

Mory heard the door shut tight. It was as though the two caretakers had been using the telephone to talk.

Martin did not remove his heavy coat when he entered the living room. All three layers of his clothing were wool. When he unbuttoned the top of his jacket, the skin around his neck looked gray. He greeted Mory and Hilda before sitting down at the edge of the sofa. He sat straight up like an athlete in training. He kept his oiled boots together and they shed a little water. He put the paper bag containing the past week's newspapers on Fred's table.

"So you're having a party?" the other caretaker asked.

"We haven't had a party in a long time," Hilda said.

"Where you having it?"

"In the boathouse."

"Be cold, won't it?"

"Roger and Suzanne are down there now," Hilda said. "They started the fire this morning and they took all the electric heaters. We'll move the liquor and pretzels in later so it don't freeze."

"Won't be cold once we get going, old boy," Fred said jauntily.

"Where's Suzanne and Roger at now?" Martin asked. He spoke slowly as though he might forget what he was saying. He had removed his gloves and was rubbing his hands. His eyeglasses were fogged.

"In the boathouse," Hilda said.

"I mean where they living at? Didn't they move awhile back?"

"Near Ithaca," Mory said. "They ain't moved."

"He working?"

"Not yet," Fred said. "He could work but I guess it's easier not to. When I was his age, it was easier to work. At least you kept alive. There wasn't none of this laying around and getting paid for it. That's what kills me. They let someone else do the work and take the handouts."

"I guess so," Martin said, nodding. "Work's scarce."

"He's having trouble with his feet," Hilda said as if to excuse Roger.

"They got the baby with them?"

"In the boathouse."

"I don't think I seen that baby, have I?" Martin liked children.

"She's real cute," Hilda said.

"Suzanne don't know how to mother her yet," Fred said. "She's terrible messy."

"She ain't got much time left to learn," Martin said, and he smiled.

"Aw, you know these kids today," Fred said. "Once they get through hanging the kids on their nipples, they store them in laundry baskets. I never seen anything like it. They don't even know how to burp them."

"She's had trouble having kids," Hilda said. "She lost two from miscarriage."

Suzanne Bettors was Hilda's youngest daughter. All six of Hilda's children were born during her first marriage. Suzanne was the last before Mory. He was the last. After her first husband deserted her, Hilda had wanted no more children and she had started being careful.

"I knew she had some trouble," Martin said kindly. "I'm glad she finally got her a baby. Well, I better be going."

"What's you rush?" Fred said. "Stick around awhile."

But he had already picked up the dictionary again.

"I got to get to the grocery store and then home. The wife wants beef and noodle soup. She takes to soup when she's poorly. Say, did you hear there's supposed to be another storm coming?"

"When, Martin?" Mory asked from deep in the lounger. He had been following every word of the conversation.

"Tonight or tomorrow, maybe. Be in West Virginia by now. Be here then, too. Probably tonight. We never seem to miss those. This one's supposed to be big."

"How big?" asked Mory.

"Bigger than you, hot shot."

"Is it?" Hilda asked. She lifted her gaze from the television set. She may have been worried about her party.

Martin stood up slowly and collected himself. Then he leaned over to touch the bag of newspapers.

"You'll want to read last Friday's, Hilda. Got a little story on Joe Ben Keller."

"What'd he do now?" Fred asked. "More trouble, I suppose."

"It was trouble but it wasn't his."

"We don't hear nothing about him. He don't come here no more. He don't want to see his mother. When he wanted money, you can bet he'd come. Probably be here again if he needs it."

Joe Ben Keller was the second of Hilda's four sons. He lived in Vermontville and the distance was great enough to make a convenient excuse not to visit Fred and Hilda. Joe Ben only worked summers and he had a wife and two noisy little children whom Fred couldn't stand. The boy had once pulled the fine tune knob off of Fred's television.

"I guess Joe Ben helped someone out of an accident," Martin said.

"At least he done something," Fred said.

"Done a good job, too. Maybe saved a life, the way they wrote it."

"At least he ain't in no more trouble."

Hilda stood up and tried to straighten her skirt. The skirt no longer fit. She was so fat from winter that her blouse was forced out in back. In places Mory could see the twin bags of parachute-white flesh that topped her hips. She came across the room and dumped the newspapers on the couch. She was looking for Friday's edition when Fred walked to the back door with Martin.

Mory lay back and moved the fingers of his right hand across his eyes. For a second he saw spots. Then he saw the cold gray Adirondack sky through his parted fingers. His fingers were still red and soft but he could move them easily.

"See you, old boy," he heard Martin say.

"Take care, old boy."

Five | Sally Anne Bettors was the ugliest child Mory had ever seen. She had nearly killed her mother being born and then spent the first two months of her life on a hospital critical list. She still had not grown enough hair and she was stuck with her father's high sloping forehead. Roger was quite bald at twenty-five but he claimed he lost most of his hair from having to wear a tight cap in the service. He was wrong. He would have lost it anyway like his father. To compensate he had let his sideburns grow.

Both Sally Anne's parents were thin but not quite thin enough to appear emaciated. The little girl was very small and she had inherited her parents' white hoselike arms and legs. Only her eyes were large. They gave her face an abnormal cast. She had a way of looking too long at certain things which interested her and she was still very much of the age when everything must be bitten. She could make a series of noises but she was unable to say any real words except her own pronunciation of daddy which she called everybody. Roger was constantly correcting her about this. He also wanted Sally Anne to walk but when she tried to stand up without someone holding her shoulders, she toppled. Then she was content to crawl. She was crawling now on the carpet. She was gradually stalking Mory's big old black tomcat Jimmy. The cat didn't mind the child because he was asleep under the table. The table held photographs of Hilda's six children, and most of her grandchildren.

Hilda was in the kitchen preparing supper.

"Did you guys get any heat up down there?" Fred asked about the boathouse. The caretaker had removed his workshoes and drawn his feet up on the couch. His white socks were brown and loose.

"Before we left, we banked the fire with the biggest log we could find," Roger said. He spoke smugly like a private reporting to a sergeant he disliked. He was smoking a cigarette against the rules.

"We'll go down and check it again before supper if you don't."

"Them electric heaters working?"

"There ain't a whole lot of outlets so we had to set up two together. The other's across by the piano."

"Will it work? I mean, does it keep the place warm?"

"I don't know, Fred. Maybe if you keep the door shut."

"I wasn't going to leave it open," Fred said. "That icebox plugged in?"

"We had to clean it first. What you been keeping in there, fish bait?"

"We thought you were going down," Suzanne said.

Compared to her husband's abrasiveness, Suzanne's voice sounded shrill. She was sitting in her mother's rocker, near Mory, with her socks up on the only footstool. Occasionally she wriggled her toes. She was chewing gum hard and watching her daughter crawl.

Fred cleared his throat. "I would have come but Martie Findle stopped by. When he comes, he don't want to do nothing but talk. I never met a man his age that was so nosy. He's got to know this and he's got to know that. He's got to know damn near everything."

"What's he want to know for?" Roger asked.

"I always liked Martin," Suzanne said. She got up to yank Sally Anne back into the middle of the room before she could touch the cat. Surprised, the little girl sat up and got her legs crossed unnaturally. She glowered at her mother who stuck out her tongue at her daughter. Roger quickly threw the girl a red rubber mouse which squeaked under pressure.

The cat hadn't moved.

"What'd he ever do for you?" Fred asked. "Something we don't know about?"

"Martin was nice, that's all," Suzanne said. This time she stuck out her tongue at Fred.

Fred ignored the tongue, something he wouldn't have done a few years before.

"He drives me and your mother nuts. Always wanting me to go over there and fix something. Why don't he fix it himself? Or pay somebody else to help? He never gave me nothing for helping him. He makes twice as much as me."

Roger inhaled and asked, "You going to put the beer in the icebox or you want me to find you a tub and fill it with snow?"

"We could do that," Fred said vaguely, as though admiring the illegal tobacco smoke. "Whatever, we decide later. It's early yet."

Hilda came to the door with a dishtowel across her arm. She didn't have anything to say. She was just checking. One of her stockings had collapsed around her ankle and they could see the sparse black hairs growing on her legs.

"How's them ribs, Ma? I feel like maybe I'll be able to try a few now. I'm feeling pretty good all of a sudden."

"They ain't ribs I'm making."

The woman had spoken carefully, as though afraid of the consequences.

Fred didn't hide his disappointment. "I thought you told me they was ribs."

"They're stew I'm making. They're that old stew meat we was saving. It'll make more."

"Stew's good, Ma, only I was looking forward to a mess of your ribs."

"We don't have no ribs," Hilda said and she went back into the kitchen silently.

Fred turned to Roger who was lighting another cigarette.

"Don't you know that's just one more nail in your coffin?"

Roger looked down at the cigarette. He was expression-less, a big masculine replica of his daughter. He brought the cigarette to his lips and exaggerated the puff. He exhaled all of it toward Fred.

Fred turned away and spoke to the wall.

"You know," the older man said, "I remember once before the war when times was hard. Depression they called it, but you kids never heard of that. We was living near Utica in this farmhouse. You probably don't even know what a farm is. It was winter like this and we didn't have no money for coffee, much less cigarettes. I wasn't working because there wasn't no jobs available. I'd of taken any job I could. It ain't like today where there's jobs everywhere but nobody willing to work. Anyhow I asked my wife, my first wife, what's she going to fix for dinner? Christ, we really didn't have no heat in the house. We was heating and cooking with wood. Wood you had to get off your damn butt and go out and chop or gather. Squaw wood was what we called what we got off the ground. She says ribs. They was deer ribs, the last of this buck I'd poached. No, I guess the last was the nose and cheeks if we got hungry enough. I remember I didn't want to go get another yet. The wardens was less strict on the rules in them days, with bread lines and people starving, but they could still hurt you for poaching. Of course, some guys wanted to be in jail on account of they had to feed you. I had a buddy like that but he didn't have no family. Anyhow that woman made those ribs last a week. We had the bones in soup before we ate them."

Fred paused, as if to verify his story with himself or the wall. He turned back and nodded toward Roger.

"It ain't easy to give up smoking."

Roger stood up and took another long puff.

"I think I'll go lay down awhile," he said. "Don't you never get tired of telling that story, Fred?"

From the lounge chair Mory watched the road. He was smiling at his brother-in-law. It would be another hour until the school bus passed. It would be the same yellow bus he had ridden since coming to the camp with his mother and sister. The same bus his brother John would have ridden if he had not been in reform school in Elmira. The same bus Suzanne had ridden until she graduated. The same damn bus he would have ridden this year if it wasn't for one cigarette. As he watched, he saw the roof of a pale green car moving along the slippery road. When the car slowed and passed the shoveled opening in the snowbank across from the mailbox, Mory turned into the room and said, "It's Luke and Loretta coming."

"Little early, ain't they?" Fred asked, as if questioning the boy's eyesight.

"It's them," Mory said. " '57 Chevrolet. Green, with a bug deflector."

Suzanne stood up and plucked her daughter off the floor.

The girl burped in her mother's arms.

"I'm going to change her," Suzanne said.

"She don't need changing," Fred said.

"I'm going," Suzanne said.

"Don't everybody leave at once," the caretaker said. "Pinsons will think we don't like them. Here, Mory, what are you going to do? Seems like everybody's doing something they don't have to do."

"I'll sit here," the boy said.

"Yeah, sit here with me," Fred said. "Old Luke might have something to say. They are early though. They might want to hit us up for dinner."

Six | The age gap between Luke and Loretta Pinson was greater than between Fred and Hilda. Luke was nearing sixty and his wife would admit forty. They had a son six months old. Because of him they were married before Christmas. They had been going together three years and Fred and Hilda stood up for them to return the earlier favor.

Luke was unbearably tall. He ducked through doorways and fit no chair comfortably. When he sat his knees were around his chin. He had a friendly face which frequently turned sad, a hard mountain visage which could lose itself in gloom when his luck ran wrong. Someday it would never come back. When Luke was drunk, he played a dandy fiddle. When he was sober, he could work hard. When he worked, he laid road asphalt for the State.

Loretta was happier to see than her husband because she was younger. For northcountry women her figure was trim. If she was not exactly trim by fashion book standards, at least she looked well under the ski outfits she usually wore during winter. Her face was nicely round and good featured and genuinely unremarkable. For the last few years she had worn her black hair very short and bobbed, as if one day with nothing to do she had climbed the attic stairs and rediscovered her high school yearbook and tried to imitate herself as a senior. Her voice was soft and smooth.

When Loretta walked into the sitting room, she was carrying the baby boy in a red canvas shopping bag borrowed from the Ames Discount Store in Saranac Lake. She sat down next to Fred and placed the boy between them. Luke sat down next to her, his head reaching almost to the shade of the standing lamp.

"How's my boy?" Fred asked and he folded back the tiny blue blanket to look at the child's face. The boy slept.

"He's a little tired," Loretta said, almost in apology.

"He's been clear to Malone today and he had more shots yesterday."

"He ain't growing much," Fred said. "You guys went to Malone?"

"Luke needed something else for his shop."

"The roads any good?"

"Pretty good."

"Where they ain't bad," Luke said. "If you stay in the ruts."

Luke had to speak into an entirely different atmosphere than the others.

"We brought you some dips and chips for tonight," Loretta said. "There's several kinds. We tried to think of something more to bring you. We're on our way home. Just thought we'd bring them now instead of later when you're busy."

The Pinsons lived beyond Tupper Lake, almost to Long Lake.

"Whyn't you stay?" Fred suggested unenthusiastically. "Ma's making stew. We was having ribs. You could eat, then you wouldn't have to go home and come all the way back."

"I'm going to dress up," Loretta said. "But we'll be back. You can bet we will." She grinned at Fred.

"You better be," the caretaker said.

For a second nobody said anything and the silence stuck until Hilda dropped a pan in the kitchen.

"We brought you a bottle of that Cream of Mint, too," Luke said.

"You did? You didn't have to do that. What'd you go do that for?"

"Seems like the least we could do," Loretta said. "You having this big party. None of our other friends has had a party in years."

"You're buying pretty fancy liquor in your old age, Pinson," Fred said, jesting.

Luke showed his smile. In the bars at Tupper some people said they could count the times on one hand when Luke Pinson had smiled.

Smiling now, Luke said, "I wonder how's come I never could develop a taste for that expensive stuff. Seems like with me, the cheaper the whiskey, the better I like it."

"Cream de Mint ain't whiskey," Fred said.

"Whatever it is."

"Hilda sure likes it. I don't care for it too much. It's O.K. for heartburn or a belly ache. For me it acts sort of like them Tums or Rollaids."

"Ain't as cheap though," said Luke because he knew.

"The boss, he had some of that Pernod once. Gave me a smell. Tastes like licorice. It's kind of yellow-green. You ever try it?"

"I tried everything, Fred. About once."

"It'll sure put hair on your eyeballs. Costs ten bucks a bottle. Big tall bottle. From France, I think, is where they make it. Or grow it. Or whatever they do."

"That's too much," Loretta said, "to put hair where you don't need it."

"I guess," Fred said. He was grinning at her.

"You being good, Mory?" Luke asked. He might have just noticed the boy. From where Luke's head was perched, he could almost look down on Mory stretched out in the corner.

"Trying to," Mory said. He had been listening to them without really hearing what they said.

"You going to be ready to go fishing with me this spring?"

"I'm ready now."

"The fish ain't."

"You done any good through the ice, old boy?" Fred interrupted.

"Not a bit. Only been twice."

"Ain't as many shacks out here this year either."

Fred considered himself an authority on all types of fishing and he had stolen the fish conversation from Mory to prove it.

"Something wrong with the ice. I been told there's lots of water underneath."

"Always is," Luke said.

He and Mory laughed out loud.

Fred spoke with a snap so he wouldn't seem the fool.

"I don't mean that. This year's different. There's water between the ice."

"Like that back in '52," Luke said. "That was a poor winter. Several people drowned."

"I guess it was. Supposed to be more snow on the way tonight."

Loretta stood up.

"That we don't need," she said. "Come on, mister. We're going home."

"What's your rush?" Fred said.

Loretta looked at him and said, "You'll be seeing all you want to see of us in a few hours, Fred Macken. And I better warn you now that I'm determined to have some fun tonight."

"You just better," Fred said, grinning again.

"What time you want us?" Luke asked.

"Whenever you get here, old boy. Be sure to bring your fiddle. Ma's got the guitar tuned and I might even have a yoddle or two left in me."

"God forbid," said Loretta.

They all laughed, including Mory.

The sky was falling swiftly into darkness. The gray slate air had turned black in the trees on the hill.

The school bus had passed unnoticed.

Seven | Before supper things became confused. The house was quieter, as though it had been insulted and would somehow retaliate. Maybe it could not handle this many people. Normally it only had to contend with Fred, Hilda, Mory, the cat, and a stray bird from Hilda's feeder who found the door open. Now it was too quiet and it was confusing, like the waiting room of a railway station at 3:00 A.M.

Originally the caretaker's house had been smaller. It had been that way when Fred lived there alone and it had been enough then. There were two small bedrooms, the bath, the kitchen, and the living room which was half porch. But as it became clear that Hilda, Suzanne and Mory were not just temporary visitors, Samuel Weaver had started making improvements. He added a big bedroom and another bath for the caretaker and his squaw. He expanded the cellar underneath the addition and punched out the living room wall to enclose the porch. He saved part of the porch for a little sewing cubicle which was a constant mess. Then in summer Weaver hired Hilda to clean the cabins and to do laundry. He also hired Suzanne to help her mother with the inside work and Mory to help Fred outside. He hired them graciously and paid them well for what they did. The children appreciated his generosity. For the first time in their lives they each had spending money.

The Weavers usually brought an ancient French cook to camp from Philadelphia. One summer she was in Dijon seeing her relatives and Weaver hired Hilda's mother to do the cooking in the main lodge. Mrs. Coulter proved a very nervous cook. She began chain smoking her cigarettes and she worried out loud that the Weavers did not appreciate anything she prepared because of their long exposure to fancy cooking. In contrast to the French cook, Mrs. Coulter's pie crusts and biscuits were wet as the first waffle, and her vegetables swam in their own brown juices, and her meats and potatoes were greasy, like the film on a bear's skinned body. Mrs. Weaver tried to reassure the cook of her skills but Mrs. Coulter stayed nervous. One morning when she couldn't find any bacon or sausage, she served hot dogs with the eggs. The guests in camp later reported this special breakfast to every open ear in Berwyn, Pennsylvania. But Mr. Weaver accepted all this graciously and his wife went along with him right through Labor Day.

After the improvements were made on the caretaker's house, Suzanne took over the bedroom closest to the old bath and Mory used the other little room across the hall. When Suzanne left to be married, her room became storage space. Yet Hilda kept the bed made and the room fairly free of cartons for visitors. Visitors were mostly Hilda's family. During the past few years the bed had slept at least twelve different persons, sometimes three at a time.

The new bedroom for Fred and Hilda at the other end of the house no longer looked new. The twin beds were left unmade because somebody was always lying down. The floor was littered with boots, clothing, newspapers without the crossword puzzles and recipes, stray pills, movie magazines with torn covers of Jacqueline Kennedy or Elizabeth Burton, fishing tackle, and pieces of sewing equipment. One of the yellow thermal curtains, bought last year to seal the room from winter like an ice chest, was already missing. A window was stuck closed with the screen still on it. The brown wall-to-wall carpeting was worn in four obvious places and every wall needed paint. Even the ceiling was spotted from leaks in the roof caused by melting ice which Fred had not bothered to chop loose.

When Samuel Weaver had inspected the room after a year's use, he graciously accepted its condition as permanent. But when he walked into the new bathroom and saw seventeen bullheads alive and swimming in the filthy bathtub, he left the house and never returned. He never knew that the fish were killed, skinned, cleaned and frozen by that night, and he never inquired and he never told his wife.

Mory's room was different. He kept it spotless. His few clothes were tucked away neatly in drawers or hung smartly in the closet. His radio was squared on the bedside table. His books, mostly mechanical, stood tall on the dresser. His two-stage Saturn rocket leaned darkly on its pad in the corner like a forgotten prototype at Cape Canaveral. The rocket worked for a thousand feet and it was his prize possession. On the floor against the only solid wall were his dumbbells, barbell, their weights, and his Sears Roebuck exercise pad which had illustrations of women's calisthenics on one side and men's on the other. Before he was hurt Mory could do the exercises at the highest men's level faster than proscribed and then top them off with weight sets. His fly rod hung on the wall over his bed and his two pairs of boxing gloves hung beneath the rod. All of Mory's possessions kept in the room were purchased with Samuel Weaver's paychecks. His room was so different from the rest of the house that it would confuse a stranger. It might have belonged to a slightly eccentric ex-professional athlete turned pilot. Except Mory was seventeen.

Hilda made efforts to pick up the living room at least once a month or for company but she had given up on the sewing cubicle. Now it represented too big a challenge for her. It was an indoor mountain of clothing, name tapes, yarn, needles, and thread. Submerged somewhere were a sewing machine and table and a high-backed wooden chair. When Hilda climbed in for something she needed, she knew there were mice underneath it all but she wouldn't tell Fred. In winter when she didn't have to worry about the Weaver boys and their torn dungarees, broken zippers, and lost buttons, she usually sewed by hand in the bedroom.

The living room had a lower ceiling than the rest of the house. The ceiling had been insulated and soundproofed because the room housed the record player, the color television, the best radio, the electric guitar and amplifying equipment, and the old spool tape recorder which Hilda had salvaged from her own house. After moving in with Fred and solving their future together, and after getting what Fred considered a reasonable offer, Hilda had sold her home in Corey's. The sale price covered her remaining payments.

Hilda was faithful to country and western music. Besides taping herself, she tried to record every good song every week from the Johnny Cash and Glen Campbell television shows, and every song from the Kraft Music Hall when Eddy Arnold was host. For these shows she would prepare the machine early and then ease herself down on the floor with the controls. Sometimes the session worked out fine but the tapes never sounded as good as the original. Some other times she got confused with the two sets of dials and wound up with nothing. When this happened or when she did not like any of the songs, were the few times when Hilda showed any emotion.

Otherwise the living room was quite simple. Stashed along with the second-hand furniture and normal debris of everyday life were Hilda's family photographs, a glass jar of jelly beans, a cracked creamer of salted nuts, an odd shoe, stacks of records without jackets, flowers and plants in pots formed as fish, and several plastic miniature white-tailed deer which were purchased as a family group and then dispersed individually to tables throughout the room. The thermal curtains were blue and the walls were bare except for a framed Winslow Homer Adirondack print of an old man in a guideboat and a large blood-red religious tapestry which Hilda had purchased as a remembrance of the shrine in Quebec where she had stayed alone for exactly thirty-six hours following the death of her second husband by drowning.

The other room in the house was the kitchen. It had not been improved because it was always all right. It was tiny but functional. There was a dishwasher near the sink, a big stove with oven, wooden cabinets on two walls and under the counter for appliances, and a formica dinette set with two extra chairs kept against the wall beneath the telephone. The table had an extra leaf which could be installed when using the additional chairs and which then backed Fred up against the icebox.

The basement was sturdy under the entire house. Hilda had her own clothes washer and dryer down there because the main camp laundry was closed in winter to keep the pipes from freezing. There was also an enormous trunk-type food freezer which Fred had bought on WNBZ's Swapshop program, and several closets for canned goods, bins for potatoes, shelves for tools and fishing tackle, and, only in winter, all the plants and flower bulbs from the camp's many outdoor pots and boxes. Mrs. Weaver loved her flowers and hated to buy them so they were kept warm through the winter by special expensive lamps. That end of the basement resembled a mad scientist's private jungle.

Hilda visited the basement regularly although every time she descended she was cautious of the wooden steps leading from the kitchen. Fred would not go down there unless he had to. He said the air was bad for his lungs and that it would kill him if it did not kill Hilda first. When he had to be in the basement to fix a pipe or the water pump which was no good, he surfaced quickly and then complained. Then he might be sick for a week.

So what should have been an easy home to keep was instead a place of neglect, laziness, spilled soap, and frequent despair. Everything usually worked somewhat but nothing except Mory's room ever looked right. Now on Wednesday evening before the party, it was a place of quiet confusion.

Just before supper John and Sara Keller arrived with their daughter, Mary. The child was asleep and her mother put her on the couch where Mory could watch her.

Hilda stood at the stove spooning Worcestershire sauce into the stew which reeked of onions. She had set the table for six, moving up the highchair for Sally Anne. She tasted the stew again and she looked tired. She would need two more chairs.

After complaining loudly that Suzanne had used up all the hot water for her baby and herself, Fred was finally bathing. They could hear him whistle and splash.

Roger snored as he slept.

Suzanne had dressed the child and now she was dressing herself. Her hair was folded in pink curlers. She pulled on her underpants and then she deliberated seriously about the appropriate color slacks to wear with her white blouse. Her long clean naked legs seemed more muscular in the weak artificial light. Her bare feet seemed longer. They were the most sensual part of her body. Her large breasts seemed soiled.

"Shit," she said, choosing the green pants.

Roger woke up and caught her half dressed and pulled her toward him.

Only Mory was completely relaxed. He lay in the lounger watching Sara's baby. He was listening to Hank Snow reciting Tales of Alaska and the Yukon on the record player. He was thinking of where he might be if he were not where he was. And if he could do anything at all about it.

Actually Mory was alive to many other places and quite dead to where he was.

Eight | Hilda's kitchen was hot. The windows were steamed. Smells clawed at the walls and climbed to the low ceiling.

Fred sat stiffly at the head of the table, waiting. His back was to the refrigerator. He wore a new shirt, open at the neck. It was green with a fine gold thread sparkling in the material, like a thin vein in the earth. His hair was dampened and combed straight back over the bald spot. He smelled sweetly of aftershave lotion.

The others took their places carefully as if the meal were questionable. On either corner at Fred's rough hands sat a small child. Their heads were no bigger than his hands. Suzanne's child was perched in the highchair and she looked down across the table at John's child who had the Columbia Encyclopedia under her for more height. Neither little girl wanted to speak. Each stared at the other seriously like forsaken women who would insult each other after eating. Their mothers sat at their sides confidently, protectively, and almost sure of their children. Roger and John sat next to their wives at the place where Roger had installed the extra table leaf. Mory sat by John near the door. His mother would sit across from him rather than at the usual opposite end of the table from Fred. Her end was flush against the window.

Hilda was loading a bowl with canned cut string beans which she then placed in front of Fred. He stirred the beans again with the spoon. They waited quietly as Hilda served up nine blue plates of stew from the steaming iron pot. She handed each plate to Fred who passed them down the table like a favor until everybody had food. There were much smaller portions for the babies. Before Hilda sat down, the bread and beans had been passed.

"It's so nice to have some of the family," Hilda said, helping herself to beans.

"Reminds me of a boarding house I stayed in one night in Troy," Fred said. He was chewing bread. "That was years ago. Night like this, too."

"We should have a grace," Sara said quietly.

John was trapped in reach for the relish jar. He withdrew his empty hand like a snake recoiling when he knows he'll get whipped. Several of them put down their forks.

"Go ahead, Sara," Hilda said. She had already bowed her head. "You say one for us."

Sara looked around the table as though frightened at what she had suggested. When her eyes met Mory's, she kept looking at him. He nodded.

"You going to say it?" John asked, without nudging.

"Say something," Roger said. "We're hungry."

"Food's getting cold," Fred said and he wrapped his forefinger on the table like one of the boys at a union hall poker game.

Suzanne laughed which burped her baby.

Then Mory nodded again at his favorite sister-in-law and he saw her eyes drop.

"Thank you, Lord, for these thy gifts which we are about to receive," Sara said softly and very quickly. Her voice was fine to hear but nearly inaudible.

"Amen, Lord," said Fred and the others echoed him in their own scattered way before digging into the sanctioned meal.

The stew was highly seasoned and good only because Hilda had made it. She had used onion in spite of Fred. All of them concentrated on eating rather than trying to talk.

They ate until the bread and beans were a memory and until the remaining stew was cold and stiff in the metal pot. For dessert they ate canned pears sprinkled with cinnamon. When the coffee perked Hilda stood up to pour it. Both babies ate well, a wipe on their mouths the only help from their mothers. Both mothers seemed surprised at their children, pleased that they were quiet, and somewhat proud, as though the eating had been a contest between them. They would settle for a tie.

When Roger and John lit cigarettes over coffee, Fred made a big production of finding them an ashtray. He insisted on going for it and he went all the way to his bedroom where he also took a leak.

When the caretaker sat down again, he said, "I missed my news tonight. Anybody catch it?" He knew nobody had.

"Probably nothing new anyway," Roger said, knowing how Fred hated to miss the evening news. Roger ignored the ashtray by flicking his cigarette over his pear dish. The ash melted black in the juice.

"That's the trouble nowadays," Fred said to nobody in particular. "People is just not informed. They don't pay attention to nothing that's happening around them. Nothing that's important. And the government can do whatever it wants."

"They would anyway," Roger said. "You can't believe what those guys tell you on TV." He knew television credibility was another of Fred's favorite topics.

But the caretaker said, "I don't know about that. Sometimes they dig up stuff the government and them don't want told. That's when it helps the little guy."

"Joe Ben made the paper last week," Hilda said. She had eaten more slowly than the rest of them and she was finishing her pears. The fruit seemed to be sloshing in her mouth as though she were blending it into something special.

"We've seen Joe Ben in town this week," John said. "He said it was a hell of a wreck."

"I'm going to send that clipping to Junior," Hilda said. Junior was her eldest son. He was a sergeant in the Army. They never heard from Junior except when he changed bases or at Christmas. He was currently stationed at Fort Benning and he didn't like cold weather so he never came to Saranac Lake. He had served in Korea and that was enough.

"We don't never see Joe Ben," Fred said.

"He looks good. He gained a little weight but you'd know him. He ain't working."

"I don't know if we want to know him," Fred said. "Why don't he come to see his mother once in a while?"

Hilda moved her chair nervously. She may have been embarrassed about Joe Ben because she took two sips of coffee, one right on top of the other, as if forgetting the first was in her mouth. She almost lost them both.

"Maybe he's busy."

"He sure ain't too busy," Fred said. He was admiring the chin of Suzanne's baby with his forefinger and thumb. When the baby wriggled her head, he let his plates slide forward in his mouth which scared her more than his hand. When he sucked his teeth back in, his mouth collapsed like a balloon. Then with a click the dentures were back again and he had a shaped mouth to drink his coffee.

"He's pretty far to come over here," John suggested.

"He ain't that far."

"Maybe something else come up."

"All winter?"

"Maybe his car don't work."

"You just said you seen him. But maybe not. I can see why. Talk about wrecks. He should know all about them. I can't understand how he gets that thing of his licensed."

"It runs good," John said.

"Well it don't look good. It ain't right."

"Maybe he'll trade it off this spring. Then he'll come over to see you."

"I hope he don't get in no rush," Fred said. "Maybe he's just too damn lazy. I swear sometimes I can't understand that kid. He don't work. At least he ain't never working. He don't do nothing. And he don't never have time to come see his mother who done everything she could for him. Just to say hello. Me and your mother bailed him out of messes more than once and that goes for you, too, John Keller. When Joe Ben needs money, then he'll come to say hello. You watch."

"We'll do the dishes, Mom," Sara said. She knew how to gauge her stepfather-in-law perfectly and she figured it was time to stop him.

"You don't have to," Hilda said. "I made the mess."

"Now, let the girls clean it up, Ma," Fred said. "You go get yourself ready. You worked too hard already today."

Hilda was unready to leave them yet.

"Anybody want more coffee?"

"Never mind the coffee. You just go get ready."

"Well, all right, I guess I will," Hilda said. She rose heavily as though this time embarrassed to be leaving, or afraid she might be missing something. Usually Hilda was afraid of nothing but blame.

"You check the boathouse?" Fred asked Roger.

"We forgot," Suzanne said, without looking at Fred. She was wiping the highchair table around her daughter's pear dish. The spilled stew had hardened and she used a knife to scrape it. It was noisy.

"All's you had to do was go look," Fred said.

"I'll go when I get ready," Roger said. "In fact I'm ready now. I need some fresh air."

"You sure didn't need any fresh air when I asked you to have a look at that truck."

"You want me to take a thermometer down there and bring you back an exact temperature?"

"Just don't get smart, fellow," Fred said. His voice had hardened. "I ain't going to horse you around. You don't have to be here."

Roger went out the door like he had to.

"You might as well go with him," Fred told John. "Give us some room to work here."

"We ain't staying for the party," John said.

"What did you come for?"

"Mom asked us."

John could handle Fred better than Roger because he had more experience.

"Yeah, well, you're staying until your wife cleans up in here," Fred said definitely.

John put on his coat and went after Roger. This time the door closed slowly because John wouldn't slam it.

Mory felt the cold air spring through the kitchen and the room changing and he followed the glow of his brother's cigarette in the window. He knew John and Roger would take a long time returning and he smiled after them.

"Come on, Mory," Fred said, "you and I'll watch the babies while their mamas clean this up."

Nine | Fred snapped on the television and sat down.

Mory took the lounger.

The babies sat on the floor exploring each other, pawing with hands and shoes, like two drunks fascinated by the next beer. Then they pawed the red mouse between them.

Jimmy the cat watched the children. Fred watched the

television. Mory watched the cat. In low artificial light the boy saw everything poorly but he could hear the girls stacking dishes.

After a while Hilda came back. She was wearing her new beige pants suit which hid most of her fat.

In January Fred had allowed Hilda to choose the suit from the catalogues. They had waited faithfully each day for the mailman to bring the order. They had built their lives around the delivery and they had not wanted the package to be left in the snow if it was too large for the box. When it finally came, the suit was the correct color but too small for Hilda's winter waist. Rather than dieting, she had made alterations. Now it fitted loosely.

"You look real nice, Ma," Fred told her. "You look like the Ma I know."

"I love this suit," Hilda said, admiring herself with her voice.

Fred looked up at her.

"It was worth it, wasn't it, Ma?"

"Ladies have these suits," Hilda said, as though she too became a lady by wearing it. As though she now had that right.

"Someday we'll get you another," Fred said. "You'll have two."

"One's enough."

"No, it ain't."

The caretaker was almost teasing her.

"A blue one," she said, imagining the blue with her voice.

"You'll be a blue jay, Ma."

"You better not shoot me, Pa."

"Any color you want. Nothing's too good for my Ma. Maybe we'll get you two more."

"They come in lots of colors."

"I thought you just wanted blue."

"Maybe the yellow would be nice."

"You already got tan. How about red?"

"What color you want me to have, Pa?"

"Whatever you want, Ma. I ain't going to wear it. I ain't got the bustline for it."

"Fred," she said to scold him gently. She saw he was smiling and that pleased her. That was as rough as she ever got with him.

"Ha, ha," Fred said, like a child laughing off his mother.

Hilda had been hiding a vanity mirror behind her back. Now she sat down on the couch and looked at herself. Her face seemed white as a Japanese dancer's. Her lips were blood red and her hair was glistening. She began to pat her hair.

"You going to the party, Mory?"

His mother's question sounded strangely grand, almost literary, and very far away, like the idea of a dress ball would sound in a slum.

Mory leaned back and forth in the lounger to make it move. The chair was like a snail walking, and going nowhere. Outside the night was black. The boy didn't answer.

"You hear me?" his mother asked. Her free hand was patting the bottom of her indian hair. Now it cupped the curled ends, her elbow out front heavily.

"Your mother's talking to you," Fred said.

Mory looked across the room at his mother. He knew about her hair and how she loved it. How once it hung down to the middle of her back. How he had clung to it as a child and followed her from room to room with nothing else to do. Then how Fred had made her cut it off after a fight when he was drunk. How Fred told her she looked like a tramp and how she cried before obeying him. Mory knew all that but he didn't know his mother's hair was dyed now to please Fred. Sometimes when she sat by the bay window and sewed in the sun, he thought he detected pieces of gray. But he would be listening to her hum and he would forget to look closely. Or when he remembered, the gray was gone.

"Mory?"

"Do you want me?" the boy asked.

"Sure we want you. Why shouldn't we want you? Grandma and Grandpa are coming. They want to see you. They'll be music and you can dance a little. I really don't know who's coming. Do you, Pa? We asked so many people. They'll be everybody you know, Mory. It'll be fun."

Hilda could hardly believe she had said so much at once. She sat back and lowered the mirror. She was nervous to be doing nothing.

Slowly Mory said, "I might come over."

"What's that mean?" Fred asked.

"I don't know," the boy said. He stretched the fingers of both hands before his face as if to count them. The eight hollow webs between his fingers were dark, like guts in a mountain side.

"Well, you know you was invited, Mory. You can't say you wasn't."

"I know."

"You know you can come," Fred said.

"Do whatever you like," Hilda said and she could not sit down any longer. A final look at her suit and she was ready to receive her guests in the boathouse.

"I'm going over now with the potato chips and paper cups."

"What's your rush?" Fred asked.

"I want to see that everything's pretty and nice like it should be."

"Can you wait for me?"

"Get the boys to help you with the drinks and the girls can bring the other food."

This was done.

Ten | Gradually the old house settled down and spread itself like an exhausted hound. Fred left for the boathouse and Hilda. John and Roger came back to carry whiskey and beer. Dinner dishes were put away. Suzanne helped carry things over and she made a second trip to retrieve her child. When John returned for the last load, Sara had moved into the sitting room with her baby and Mory. It was a room very much at peace.

"We ready to go?" Sara asked.

"Let's stay," John said.

"We can't."

"For a little while we can. Just to see who comes and how it goes. Then we'll leave."

Sara spoke to the walls. "Just to have a drink," she said.

Sara did not use alcohol and she had known John to drink badly. More than once.

John was slightly irritated. He had to pause before he could say, "Nobody ever told me I can't drink. Not yet."

"No," Sara said, not looking at her husband. "But you do have to work tonight."

"If I had to, I could work drunk."

It was more boast than statement of fact.

"I know."

"Then what's the bitch?"

"There isn't any. I just don't want there to be."

"There won't be, but we're staying."

"You said we weren't staying."

"I just said we were," John said. "I've changed my mind. You coming to the party?"

"I'm staying here with Mory until you want to go," the girl said. There was a fine unchipped edge to her voice.

"Christ, Sara, I don't have to be to work until eleven. It's only eight. We'll leave by nine."

"Whenever you're ready," Sara said. "Just as long as we leave. And as long as you know I don't want to stay."

"You want the car keys?"

"No, I don't want the keys."

"Look," John said, but he didn't want to argue with his wife because when he looked at her, he saw everything he most wanted.

"I'll just go pump Roger for a bit before I go pump the gas for you."

"O.K.," she said. It was a delicate balance.

"It is all right?" John asked, having second thoughts.

"It's all right, John," Mory said coolly. He was not looking at his brother either. His voice flowed smoothly from the dark corner, seeming to make it all right for John to join the party, like a high order being rescinded.

They heard John struggle with the last of the beer cans in the kitchen before they heard the door slam the final time. Then Sara came over and sat at Mory's feet where she could watch her child. Sara was also out of the light.

Sara Keller was a lovely young woman. Without makeup her face was as fine as any treated poster girl's. Her face was perfectly balanced and soft and big-eyed always. Her eyes were gray, holding all her mystery without giving any of her away. She could keep her emotions inside. Everything about her seemed to have been ordered and designed specially. The delivery was a treasure. Her figure was young and perfectly lean, like a strong colt just grown to fullness. The baby had not damaged her anywhere. Her long gracious hair was black as coal cleansed by rain and her hands were strong and understanding like a nurse's. Sara dressed tastefully and consciously within her budget but she could have made a soiled sweatshirt fashionable outside the gymnasium, and cause for jealousy. She was a complete person, smart enough to win scholarships in high school and to have gone on to college, had she not married John. She was good to her husband, strict to her child, and more than any of this to Mory, who was terribly fond of her.

For a while Mory watched Sara watching her child. He was not trying to feel what went on between them but it was warm. The baby was walking hesitantly toward her mother. The little girl came closer and then she reached out and grabbed her mother's thin turtleneck sweater at her left breast. It was like a signal. Sara removed the tiny hand and pulled the child into her more closely. She kissed her daughter on the head, as if the kiss were sacred, and then she held the child in both arms. The baby was good and steady and quiet.

"Looks like you've got my niece in check," Mory said. Now he was watching the first cars arrive out on the highway. Through the window the glare of their headlamps looked like field spotlights sweeping a perimeter, blinding the last enemy gunners, and picking out the dead. The battlefield was yellow.

"She's never any trouble, Mory. She minds."

"She's something like her mother," Mory said.

"That's the nicest thing I've heard all day," Sara said. She reached up and patted Mory's right hand. When he withdrew his hand from under hers, she asked, "Did I hurt you?"

"You can't hurt me," he told her. He was talking to the back of her head.

"No," she said nodding. "You're the one person I couldn't hurt. Besides, you've been hurt enough."

"Sometimes I don't feel hurt," Mory said. "Other times

I know I can never get out from under my hurt. It's not pain. That's all gone now, most of it. It's not what happened under the ladder. It's just everything that's ever happened. Everything I've ever known. Like in a book. And it's so heavy sometimes, the way snow feels when you're already wet."

"You're not old enough for thoughts like that," Sara told him nicely, but she was understanding him.

"How old do you think I am?"

"You're seventeen. At least that's what you're supposed to be."

"No, I'm not."

She almost lost him but she asked, "How old do you think you are?"

"Oh, I don't know but I know I'm older than I'm supposed to be."

"Mory Keller, what on earth are you talking about?" He had caught her interest and she smiled.

"I'm old enough to be married and to have my own children."

Sara's eyes danced in the darkness. She hugged her daughter, whose eyes were closed. The baby was standing in her arms but its body was asleep.

"Someday you'll be married, Mory."

"I don't want to be married."

"You don't have to be."

"Maybe I won't be."

"I bet you will, though. It means a lot."

"It doesn't mean anything," Mory said sharply. He knew he could tell Sara anything and she would keep it.

"It just means more hurt."

She looked up at him and asked, "What about the girls you know in school? They don't hurt you, do they?"

"They can't," he said, "but I don't want any of them. I

don't want anything to do with them. Sure, they do things but I don't want to do them with them."

"You will, Mory. You'll find a girl you want to do everything with. She'll be your wife."

"Was it that way with you and John?"

"I guess," she said, "it really was."

"John used to tell me things."

Sara leaned back into the chair so Mory had to move his legs.

"What did he tell you?"

Sara wasn't a curious person and she wasn't worried about what he might say. She didn't need to know anything more about herself than she already knew.

"I don't know," Mory said.

"If you remember, then you know. You can tell me."

Mory turned his head to watch another car arriving. He caught the lights far down the road at the first bend and he stayed with them until they had passed and the window was black again. Then he spoke to the glass.

"I do know. John told me things that made me want to be him. I never wanted to be anybody else except Farrish Miller."

Farrish Miller built guideboats for profit in Saranac Lake. He did everything else for himself. He was well known as an individual but seldom seen. In the summer he emerged from his shop to win every canoe or guideboat race he entered either on lakes or white water. Although he was not a large man, he was powerful and he was a craftsman and he was kind to people he liked. Miller let Mory visit his shop whenever the boy wanted and he answered all his questions and even showed him the scars from his shrapnel wounds. Once he gave Mory a canoe paddle which wasn't perfect enough to sell and Mory kept it in his room with his other treasures. He never let anyone else use the paddle. Then in a hurry Mory had left it in the Weavers' boathouse and one of the guests had lost it on the Racquette River. He had never told Farrish the paddle was missing. In his mind it really wasn't. He could still feel the handle give in his grip and the smooth strong yet playful strokes the blade made and the growing aches at the top center of his back. Mory had never wanted to be anyone else but Farrish Miller.

"What else did John tell you about me?" Sara asked, bringing him back.

"Where you used to go together."

"Yes."

"And what you used to do."

"All of it?"

"Yes, and then sometimes at night we used to talk about how badly Fred treated you. What he used to call you. God it used to make John mad. I'd get mad too. Shaking mad. What made me maddest was Mom not stepping in to help. Fred saying those things he didn't know."

"Maybe she couldn't help, Mory."

"She was just as bad. I know that. She can't help what she's like. She never could."

"Oh, Mory," Sara said, turning around again, "you know too much and it's all there inside you."

"It's black stuff," the boy said.

"No," Sara said. "It's white. Like a clean sheet."

"It is?"

"When it comes out."

"I think I used to get madder than John."

"What did they say about me?"

"Didn't John ever tell you?"

"You tell me."

Mory sat up.

"Can I really tell you? You won't mind?"

"I won't mind."

"I don't like this," Mory said, as though he were about to tread on water.

"Go ahead."

"Remember when John gave you that coat you wanted for Christmas? The skin parka? The one you always wear?"

"Yes, I'm wearing it tonight. It's in the car."

"I think that made Fred maddest. Like he gets when he sees a bear. I don't know why he hates bears. But that's what I remember best. Fred couldn't stand to have John give you a forty dollar coat and only give Mom a pot or something cheap. But what made him more mad was John only gave him a rabbit's foot key chain from Newberry's."

Sara began to laugh.

Mory went on. "It was only a little foot, too. And it was dyed pink."

"Just what he always needed," Sara said and she was laughing. "For luck."

"I guess it never worked. But that's not the worst of it."

"That's not bad at all," Sara said, still laughing.

"Fred said he could tell by your eyes that you were fucked out."

Sara's mouth snapped like a trap but Mory didn't stop.

"He said all you ever did for John was to get him out of work and suck him into pool halls and then screw him dry."

For a while Sara was breathing the entire room. When she'd had enough, she said, "Sounds like he didn't think too much of me." She could not have laughed again.

"He said your mother was a drunk."

"He said a lot, didn't he?"

"He always does. You want to hear more?"

"No."

"It was never fair. I knew that."

"Did you stick up for me, Mory?"

"I did," he said. "Yes, I did. But I never told John."

"What did they say when you stuck up for me?"

"They didn't know you were so good," the boy said

quietly. Mory had not been seeing any more lights on the road.

"Have they hurt you, too?"

"I guess so. But they can't help it. They're old. I know that. The only thing that really bothers me is falling behind."

"In school?"

"Everywhere. Just by being out here I fall behind. It's like a trap. Ask John. Ask Suzanne. They'll both tell you. They left as soon as they could."

Sara nodded and said, "You'll just have to catch up."

"When I can."

"Yes."

"Sara?"

"Yes."

She was watching him now.

"Can I tell you something else?"

"Sure you can. Anything."

At first no words came. Mory made a long pause, leaving a hollow between them. Then he said, "The only time I didn't feel trapped was when I was on fire."

Mory might have wanted to say something else then but John came into the house in a hurry. His eyes looked a little wild.

"Snowing," John said. "We got to go."

Sara stood up with the baby.

"You all right?"

"Yeah, I'm all right. But this whole goddamn place drives me nuts. You should see the party they're having. Talk about your dingbats. Fred's pickled already and he usually don't show it this early. Did you ever hear that bastard yoddle? You want to go see it before we go?"

"I don't think so," Sara said.

Then, still holding her baby, she leaned over and kissed Mory above his right eye, where the skin was purple.

"What's that for?" John asked, wavering slightly.

Sara did not answer him.

"Come and see us, Mory," she said. "Come whenever you want."

Eleven | Through the window Mory watched them go. It seemed as though John's car were standing still and his chair were moving backward. He held on. He had not forgotten them yet and Sara's kiss but they were only the twin red taillights of the new second-hand Mustang coupe.

Fred had said the Mustang was too sporty and that John didn't need it. He said it made too much noise, had low clearance, no room inside, and too much engine. According to Fred the Mustang was a car which "John couldn't tell nothing about," which had probably been "wrecked at least once," and which was "too much cost for what you're going to have to give for it." The debate had lasted a week before John bought the car. Now it held the family, just a pair of taillights slipping past the bend. Then the car was gone and night remained darkly of them for Mory, another journey beginning from this place.

Mory smiled. He was thinking how Fred abused cars. The caretaker drove too fast and each year he seemed to drive closer to the white line and his reflexes were failing. Sometimes he drank before driving. When Hilda rode with him she was speechless until they stopped. She sat straight up way over on her side of the front seat, like a babysitter being taken home. Or sometimes she inched into the middle, like a teenager's date, holding her purse with her knees, and watching the road for Fred. Hilda looked for things Fred could not see or might miss, like death when it tried to come. And Fred would be hunched over the steering wheel and peering through his hands and he would be whistling to himself. Mory could see them now, rolling on the road.

Before Christmas the Mackens had gone to Utica to visit Hilda's older daughter, Carmen, whose husband dealt in junk. Starting back one morning after a severe snowstorm, they had collided at an intersection.

According to Fred later, "It was the old woman's fault. She couldn't see nothing."

The caretaker had tried to go around the woman's stalled car but he had hit her broadside.

Now the two-door white Pontiac which the Weavers had bought new for them was buried beneath five feet of snow at a Utica gas station. Carmen's husband was going to do something about the car but by any insurance company's appraisal which Fred cared to get the car was a total wreck. And now the Mackens drove a blue 1967 four-door Buick sedan, air conditioned for the winter.

Mory heard all about the collision but he had stayed home. He had seen his mother return with the bad knee and the black swollen eye. Later he had heard Fred complain of the pains in his back which forced him to lie down.

"She was standing there in the snow screaming with the blood gushing down her face," Fred had told the boy so he could imagine his mother better. "I thought she was dead."

Now when Mory looked, there were no cars on the road. Jimmy the cat came over and jumped onto the chair, his black body light as a leaf tossed by wind. The big cat strolled confidently along Mory's leg until he reached his stomach. There he sat down facing the boy. Mory stroked the bony ridge of Jim's back. The cat purred. The boy always let Jimmy do whatever he wanted.

"I don't know about you, tough," Mory told the cat.

"But I'm going over to the party. You don't mind, do you, James? I let you go wherever you want. Only I really don't want to go. Only I'm going."

The boy eased up slowly, chasing the cat onto the rug.

As Mory rose he felt he had lived his whole life in the chair and he wanted to be rid of it. He stood up and walked down the hall to his room and he got his ski parka off the hanger in the closet. It was an old green down parka with ski patches on the sleeves from every run in the Tri-Lakes. Mory valued it far above its worth. He put on the jacket over his white sweater and zippered it tight around him. When he pushed his hands into the pockets to fill them out, he discovered his red headjock which still had a Whiteface tow ticket stapled to it from last year. He left the headgear behind on the bed.

A light crystal snow was falling on the wooden boardwalk to the driveway. There wasn't enough snow yet to be slippery and in the light from the kitchen door it almost looked to be raining. Mory did not bother to count the cars in the driveway but there were seven. Each had a film of snow. When he walked out of the light he felt a breeze and he put his hands in his pockets.

He walked past the garage and the pumphouse where they stored the garbage cans. The summer laundry stood darkly to his right, with the open woodpile at one end and the extra maid's bedroom at the other. The camp buildings were painted brown. He walked down the winter road which Fred plowed over the back lawn to get the oil delivery truck to Weaver's cabin at the far end. This makeshift road disappeared with the snow. It was the only avenue which Fred kept plowed except the service drive. Whereas the service drive curled quickly back toward the garage and Fred's house on the highway, the main driveway went straight ahead toward the lake. It stopped short of the boathouse to make a similar curve toward the lodge. The two drives were a pair of dirt L's, one set over the other, with the main hook at the bottom nearest the lake and impossible for Fred to plow. Whenever the Weavers were away, the bottom hook was sealed off with a sawhorse to bar picnickers and snowmobilers.

Where Fred had made the access lane the snow was perhaps four feet and the bank was higher on the right, the cabin and lake side. On the left was the garden fence and the white pine and birch forest which hid the camp from the highway.

The garden was interesting. Fred had begun to build it shortly after he began to slow down. It was as though from then on he would be content to let any of his energy drain into the earth. Frequently it excited him.

The garden was Mrs. Weaver's idea. She suggested it and her husband bought a little John Deere tractor with the necessary attachments and then helped Fred cut down four big trees to clear the area. The first year the garden flopped. The deer ate everything. Then Fred put up the fence and the soil improved and he was planting confidently and growing vegetables as nice as any available in town. The Adirondack growing season was just long enough to make a garden worthwhile and there was plenty of rain. Eventually the garden produced enough vegetables each year to satisfy the Weavers and enough were left over for Hilda to freeze or can.

Yet Fred insisted there should be more. He claimed the Weavers' French cook was giving away his vegetables to anybody she pleased. He said she acted like she owned the garden and he complained she stepped on his peas when she went out to pick. He said she wasted other food.

Mory knew different. He knew the Weavers' cook as a kindly woman who read her Bible faithfully, who needed to stoop when she walked, and who genuinely loved the Adirondacks when she wasn't cooking. Mory thought she was generally more aristocratic than the Weavers and always more appreciative of the mountain surroundings. He saw how she handled Fred by ignoring him and how she kept his mother out of the lodge. The cook slept in a small room at the back of the building near where Mory was walking now. And she was always good to him. She invited him into her kitchen and gave him fresh cakes and cookies, but she would not tolerate either Macken.

For a week after Labor Day when Fred and Hilda closed the main camp, they would discuss the Weavers' cook and the bad things she'd done that summer. The garden would still be high. Then they would go buy their apples and the usual poor side of beef from a relative in Onchiota. They bought the beef so Fred wouldn't have to shoot a deer and dress it for their winter meat supply. He could shoot one in the garden from the bathroom window.

Now Mory walked behind the main lodge which was the largest building and the hub of summer activity. He thought he could detect where the snow shoveled from the roof had built up near the back door. He thought he might be able to climb up the snow right onto the roof if they had to shovel again.

Mory walked between the two extra guest cabins and went on until he reached the Weavers' own cabin where the plow had stopped. There was no light in any of the summer buildings or from the sky but he could see vaguely by the snow. He turned toward the lake, climbed onto the bank, and dropped over onto the open space where another guest cabin had been removed to have a lawn for croquet. The crust held him and he walked to where he knew the boardwalk was. He turned another right and came up the front of the camp along the screened sleeping porches like a guest. When he reached the closed windows of the lodge dining room, Mory visualized the huge wooden table and sixteen high-backed chairs which made the room seem like a court. The Upper Saranac Lake was frozen to his left but he could not see any of it through the trees. Nor could he see the hump of the barbecue area where the Weavers served their summer picnics and broiled immaculate trembling steaks over wood fires, so the smells rose to the treetops and drifted toward the highway. He could not see very much of anything but he knew where everything was.

When he reached the library at the end of the lodge, Mory saw lights through the trees from the boathouse. He heard his mother imitating Chickie Williams with "Wildwood Flowers" and how she went directly into "The Old Brown Coat and Me" without missing. The white pine trunks seemed enormous around him and he felt the tinsel snow on his face and heard it falling faintly but he did not feel cold. He stopped and stood still, seeing his breath, listening to his mother's voice, and to her strong fingers as they found the electric guitar strings. He heard the fiddle jumping in Luke Pinson's hands and someone playing the old untuned piano which sounded like a banjo. When the set ended, he heard clapping, whistling, and even a war whoop.

Then Mory wanted to go back to his room rather than to the party but he heard another voice which he recognized as a Carl Smith recording. Feeling a chill like excitement, the boy turned toward the lights, still walking on crust.

Twelve | The Weavers' boathouse was built on two levels over the high bank at the edge of the lake. It leaned toward the water. At the bottom the boathouse was built into the bank with a concrete wall. The front was open. There were three shaped slips for powerboats but Weaver only owned two, a short Chris-Craft inboard speedboat for water skiing and a slower fourteen-foot aluminum outboard for lake trout fishing and general use. The outboard motor and speedboat were taken to Lake Saranac each fall for overhaul and winter storage. The aluminum boat was pulled onto the wooden floor behind its slip and turned over. In winter the water in the slips did not freeze completely because Fred's ice machine worked constantly. The machine was an electric compressor which pushed air through three-quarter-inch pipes set in a rectangle on stones out in the water. The air escaped through holes drilled in the pipes at intervals and kept the ice from forming.

On the lower level there was also a room with a sliding door which opened onto a short concrete dock where there was a ramp into the water in summer. Here Weaver stored his canoes and guideboats upside down off the floor on wooden arms. The oars and paddles were racked against one wall, blades down, like cooking utensils in a kitchen. Beneath them were piles of water paraphernalia such as rubber swim fins and diving masks, old fiberglass trolling rods, white blocks of flotation, plastic gasoline jugs, and those heavy useless life preservers which double as cushions. Several wooden folding chairs had gradually worked their way down from the main camp and were now used by Fred and Hilda for summer bullhead fishing off the dock. There was an iron standing lamp with an extension cord and no shade which the couple used to see by when they fished.

Behind the boat slips near the wall was an open stairway leading to a trapdoor in the floor of the rumpus room above at ground level. This huge room held the party. It was beautifully paneled. It had a stone fireplace and a high beamed ceiling which bats loved. Where there were not windows, there was enough room for a collection of stuffed African animal heads which had been in the boathouse when Weaver bought the camp. Very old and heavy, and quite impossible to clean now, the animals were so badly mounted it was difficult to imagine any of them ever having lived. Each head had a small brass plaque at the base of its neck where the skin ended to describe what it was. Some of them were wrong.

Mrs. Weaver always detested the trophies. After she first examined them, she tried to locate another spot for them but there was little room for storage at the camp. Then she tried to give them away but nobody near Saranac Lake wanted to own a forty-year-old collection of African animal heads with the hair rubbed smooth over the cracked skin, the eyes set wrong, cobwebs in the horns, and dust in the ears. Weaver was rather fond of them so the heads had stayed there to guard the room.

Outside over the lake was an open porch with a railing. At the edge of the railing hung empty wooden flower boxes which were painted each spring and filled with geraniums. The railing worked.

When Mory came into the boathouse, Suzanne was placing a Kitty Wells record on the machine. She decided she didn't like what she was hearing so she skipped the arm over a couple of grooves. The volume was turned up so there were loud groans until Suzanne left the machine alone.

When Mory looked around, people seemed to be everywhere. Many of them he didn't recognize. They were all ages. Mostly the youngsters were on the floor and the adults were in chairs or standing.

To make the dance floor, the throwrug was rolled back against the sofa. People had to step over it so the couch was empty. The chairs had been pushed around at random, leaving the wooden floor open like a stage. The ping pong table was folded up against the far wall near the piano but the pool table, which had a heavy wooden cover, was serving as the bar. The top was littered with cans, bottles, paper cups, and puddles where they had spilled. There were bowls of pretzels and potato chips, and tins of dip, and jars of mustard and relishes, and open packages of weiners to roast on the wood fire, and greasy bags of rolls to put them in. Everybody including the kids looked drunk. Or, if they couldn't all be drunk, at least they looked confused.

Fred was talking to Luke near the icebox. The icebox door was open and it was crammed with cans of beer and pop. Fred was holding his cup at an impossible angle so whenever he moved his hand the whiskey spilled. When this happened, Luke moved back unsteadily.

Hilda sat near the piano with the throat of her orange guitar sticking up between her legs. Cups were scattered around her feet. She seemed to be studying the lone ice cube which was melting on the floor near her right shoe.

A woman whom Mory had never seen before was sitting on the piano stool with her elbows on the keys. She was wearing boots and she had bumps on her face. Luke's fiddle lay on top of the piano.

Kitty Wells sang loudly. Everyone else spoke just as loudly, as though they all really had something to say. Nobody could have been listening. Tobacco smoke hung over the party like a ground fog in a high peaks gully. Only it was stale.

Mory's grandparents were sitting rigidly on two captain's chairs near the empty couch. At the moment they were the only people who weren't speaking, as if they alone were waiting for something great to happen. When Mory went across the dance floor to them, he had to step over children and to be careful of their soda cans.

"Why, here he is," Mrs. Coulter said, seeing Mory. She held out her left hand because she needed her right to smoke. Mory's grandmother was a heavy woman like his mother, but her face was shrivelled down. Her legs were swollen beneath her stockings and she had no visible ankles.

She was straight fat leg from her heavy knees to her brogans.

Mory shook hands left handed.

"You come to sit with us," she said. Her voice was husky and she turned toward her husband.

Mr. Coulter did not speak or move. A tall man with the veins showing in his face, he sat stiffly and stared at the fire. He held his cold chewed pipe in his gnarled hand like a dimestore carving. Mory could tell he was drunk.

"You been missing the party, Mory," his grandmother said. Her body swayed faintly to the Kitty Wells ballad, like an old hooker remembering. "It's been a nice party. Real nice. Everybody having fun. The nicest party I remember. Where you been?"

"Talking to Sara," Mory said.

"Where's your sister?"

"She's there," Mory said, pointing to Suzanne across the room. Suzanne had her arm around Roger as if she'd decided to keep him.

"Not that one. Sara, I mean."

"She's gone home. Johnny had to work."

"What's the matter? We didn't never see her, Mory. Don't she like us?"

"She likes you. They just had to go."

"Why don't she go to the party then?"

His grandmother was trying to be careful with her words but she was having difficulty. Her hand trembled when she put out her cigarette and lit another. She smoked like a man and the fingers of her right hand were yellow. Mory could always smell the tobacco in her clothes.

"Maybe she doesn't like parties," the boy said.

"Maybe she don't," Mrs. Coulter said nodding. "Maybe not."

Mory watched a child crawl up to touch his tennis shoes.

"Where's that?" his grandmother asked, looking down at the child.

"Where's what?"

"I mean whose baby boy is that? There's just too many of them."

"I don't know," Mory said, letting the boy play with his shoe until he yanked the lace.

"Did you want another drink, Mory?"

"No."

"Did you hear that your brother got famous?"

"Did you read the story?"

"I don't like the winter anymore," Mrs. Coulter said. "I used to like the winter but I don't like them anymore. There's been too much winter now."

"Did you read about Joe Ben?" Mory asked to bring her back.

"When I met your grandfather, it was winter then," the old woman said. "It was all winter."

Mory lifted his foot to tie the lace. The child was crawling back toward the fireplace, like a nosy bear cub. The flames were blue under the logs.

When his grandmother was like this, Mory could ask her the color of the sky and she might describe turnips.

"Where's Joe Ben?" she asked suddenly. She may have been coming back.

"He's home."

"Joe Ben's home, Harry," she told her husband. The old man didn't even nod. His eyes were all of him that moved. But it was not normal movement. It was something deep inside of him moving and it only moved because of the whiskey and music.

"I don't know why Joe Ben," Mrs. Coulter said.

"Why he what?"

"I guess I do know. It's just that my silly memory's no good no more."

Mory knew better than to help her remember. Once sprung her memory was endless.

But he asked, "Why what, Grandma? You were saying something about Joe Ben."

"He don't like parties," she said.

"He just couldn't come. That's all."

"Did he say that?"

"I didn't talk to him."

"But I know why," she said. "And you know what? I even heard they was going to close the bobsled run early this year. Can't stand too much winter."

"Where'd you hear that?"

"Maybe I didn't hear. Harry told me." She looked at her husband. The cigarette ash hung long at her fingertips. She looked defeated.

"They're finished for the year anyway," Mory said. "The run was supposed to close."

"They're not finished if I don't say so. I been here too long. But I bet it's because she don't like parties."

"Who, Grandma?"

"Sara that Joe Ben married. She wouldn't even come see her grandmother at the party. What kind of wife is that for a girl? Joe Ben should know better. His mother told him better. And Fred did. I heard Fred."

Mory began to explain. "Sara is John's wife."

"Yes, but she should know better. I know better."

"John had to work."

"Don't mean Joe Ben did, too. He could have come without her."

"His wife's Mary."

"She should have come, too."

"Grandma, they live a long way from here."

"It don't matter," Mrs. Coulter said. "But it was a terrible thing."

"What was?" Mory asked. He knew she might be thinking about the death of a Soviet cosmonaut.

"The wreck," Mrs. Coulter said.

"But Joe Ben wasn't hurt."

Mrs. Coulter held onto her cigarette until it burned her fingers. Mory watched it smoke and he wanted to take it from her but she dropped it.

When he picked the cigarette up for her, she said, "Now see, Mory. They're going ready to play again and Hilda looks so pretty and plays so nice. You want to watch your little daughter, Harry."

She nudged her stone-faced husband and knocked him sideways in the chair.

Thirteen | Luke Pinson grinned as he picked his way across to the piano. He swapped his drink for the fiddle and tucked the instrument into his chin. He leaned over and spoke to Hilda. He was holding the fiddle with his neck.

Hilda was adjusting the strap of her guitar. She had removed her suit jacket and her blouse was pulled out around her waist. Her breasts seemed lower. She nodded at Luke and then fussed with the amplifier. Her fingers picked at the strings over the hole but they produced no noise. Looking foolish, she stopped to readjust the amplifier.

Several guests who were ready to dance laughed but the others stood patiently on the open floor. Their knees were bent slightly. They held each other and watched Hilda fumble.

Very flustered, she removed the strap again which wasn't necessary. Luke told her something to make her smile. The woman sitting behind at the piano was poised, her hands suspended above the keys, her eyes fixed on the music rack, as if it held a sheet.

Then Hilda began again, the sounds arriving firmly, then faltering, then strong again, her hands working together, her eyes down on her crossed legs, concentrating. Luke joined her with the fiddle. His arms were high, elbows out, the bow challenging the field of strings. And the woman behind picked them up on the keyboard, still reading the music that wasn't there. One of her booted feet pumped at the floor from the high revolving stool. Then she was with them smoothly and the guests were dancing in a different room, newly filled and rearranged by "The Old Brown Coat." When they all got together, the music was clean and lively and their dancing feet rose high off the floor in calculated confident halfsteps. Now they heard Luke alone. Now Hilda stringing out. Then the piano sounding tinny and labored. They were all together and the children and onlookers were laughing as the dancers threw back their heads, like horses going home under tight reins. The room turned carousel with the music and it began to sway and bob and rise even.

"Whyn't you dance, Mory?" Mrs. Coulter asked, moving her clasped hands over her knees to the happy music. "Whyn't you see?"

"Who'll I dance with?" Mory asked. They both had to raise their voices to hear each other.

"Why me," Mrs. Coulter said and she stood up and took Mory by the hand to lead him into dancing.

He pulled back, nearly throwing her. "I can't dance with you." But she tugged him.

"Nonshit," she said, slurring her new word. "I could dance with my grandmother. Look at them." She pointed at two eleven-year-old girls who were dancing together.

Mory tried to resist and he would have won had Fred not emerged behind his back to push him.

"Go on, Mory," Fred urged. "Show the old bastard how."

Mrs. Coulter laughed.

The band slid into "Maplewood Sweetheart." The change was barely noticeable. Now other couples were dancing and the small kids danced in groups.

Holding his grandmother at a distance, Mory felt the hardness of her back and the crispness of her party dress under her sweater. His own back was rigid, his shoulders slumped under her heavy hand, his leading arm locked with hers. They began to turn. They caught the rhythm and they went faster. He had never danced well and he knew it. They began to bump other couples who gave way or stopped to look at them, smiling nicely. People said things. The floor spun under Mory's feet and he seemed to move over it without touching. When he looked in at his grandmother, she was talking to him but he couldn't hear her voice above the electric guitar. She seemed to be holding onto him too tightly, like someone scared in a roller coaster. Her eyes only opened when she dared them to. Yet she was smiling. He went faster, forcing the old woman to stay with him, and not caring. The ceiling spun to meet the floor and he thought he heard Fred or Roger speaking, and then he felt his grandmother slip and going and he caught her with his right arm and brought her back with his left and spun her again, heaving like a log slipping.

"Can't take no more," she said.

"You got to, Grandma. You asked for it."

"Was it?" she asked in disbelief as he spun her again. "Mory, please, for my sake."

Then he saw she was going to be sick and he stopped. The music changed abruptly, nearly vanishing, and Mory heard his mother begin "Crazy," the Patsy Cline favorite. He led his grandmother back to her chair carefully, as though afraid to be too close to her anymore. He knew he had exhausted her intentionally but he didn't know why. When finally Mory sat down on the arm of the couch to catch up with himself, he was sweating.

Fred turned off half the overhead lights as Hilda tried to give the sad ballad weight. Now fewer people were dancing. Luke was at his cup again, the fiddle perched under his elbow.

"You done good, Mory," Mrs. Coulter said. "But I ain't going to dance with you no more. You too young for me, Mory. We showed them but I ain't as old as I used to be."

"You're all right, Grandma," Mory said.

"That's right," she said. "Did you see us, Harry?"

The old man nodded and his chin dropped to his chest.

"We was a sight," she told him.

Then Mr. Coulter spoke.

All he said was, "I'll be a sight, too."

Then he collapsed.

Mr. Coulter's head fell first, hard onto the floor at his feet. It made a hollow sound when it struck. For a moment he was hung up between his head and knees, like a short bridge. Then he fell back onto his side and his long legs gathered themselves in, like a child trying to sleep. Then some woman yelled. The music had stopped before she finished yelling.

Neither Mory nor his grandmother moved. She had only gasped. She was looking at her husband's body as though she had never known it.

"He's happened," she said and a circle of people closed around them. They were all ages, all disbelieving.

Fred pushed his way to the center. He was shouting. When he reached the older man, he knelt down and felt his chest.

"Still breathing," he said, looking up into faces.

"Watch the tongue," said a man.

"He ain't having no fit," said a woman.

Then Hilda burst into the circle. She was crying terribly.

"Stay away," Fred warned her. She watched as Fred pried open Mr. Coulter's mouth and reached in with a forefinger. His finger poked around and then came out with a set of dentures which his hand held up like a trophy.

Several children stepped back.

"Better call the Rescue Wagon," a man suggested importantly.

"Yeah," Fred said, examining the teeth as though mesmerized by what he was doing.

"Can he sit up?"

"Don't try to move him."

"Where's a phone?"

"I'll go."

"No, you stay here."

"He's going to be all right, Hilda."

"Somebody go, damnit."

Fred looked up and said, "Roger, quit your standing around with your finger up your ass and get on the phone." Then the caretaker rolled Mr. Coulter onto his back and yanked on his legs to straighten them. Someone brought a cushion for his head.

The old man looked dazed but happy. He was smiling and his throat moved as he breathed. His blue lips were still.

Fred gave the teeth to Mrs. Coulter and leaned over her husband's head until his ear was on the old man's mouth.

"Yeah, he's breathing," he said.

"Well, don't shut her down."

"Heart," someone said.

"Rub his heart, Fred."

Fred began to rub the chest. He looked away, as though doing another's laundry.

"Go under the shirt, Fred."

He unbuttoned the heavy wool shirt and massaged inside.

Mrs. Coulter held the teeth with both hands.

"It's Harry's heart," she told Mory. "He had such a good heart." Unlike her daughter, she was not crying.

"He ain't dead yet," Fred said. "Hilda, quit your goddamn bawling. Now everybody get out of here. Go home. The party's over."

Guests began to trickle out, their heads bowed, pushing their kids. It was as though Mr. Coulter were dead already and they had paid their respects. A few of the men came over near Mory but he did not look at them.

"What happened?" one asked.

"He just fell over," Mory said, remembering how it was.

"Must have got overexcited."

"Will you quit your talking, Benny?" Fred yelled. "Quit asking the boy questions. He don't know no more than you."

Fred was still massaging but he only used one hand now.

"Mory, take your mother and grandmother up to the house."

"I want to stay," Hilda said.

"Do as I say."

"I ain't going. I'm staying with Pa."

"You ain't going to help none, Hilda."

"I ain't leaving."

"All right, goddamnit, stay."

Roger came back breathing hard. There was fresh snow on his sweater and the old snow clung to his knees where he had fallen in. He said he'd telephoned. The fire department was on the way.

"Then get the hell back out in the road and wait for them," Fred said.

"I'll go with you," Suzanne said. They looked glad when they left together.

Mory had slipped over onto the couch. When he looked down at the floor, his grandfather looked no different. He thought the old man had merely grown too tired, but he had never seen him asleep before.

The Rescue Wagon driver parked near the woodpile. Most cars had left and it was snowing heavily. The driver and the orderly were both volunteers. They had to slide the stretcher over the old snow. It was a ski patrol basket stretcher and it slid easily, even with the oxygen cylinder.

The orderly immediately cupped the oxygen to the old man's face. The driver and the few men who stayed carried the stretcher inside the boathouse. No one said much. When they lifted Mr. Coulter into the stretcher and folded the blanket over him, his leather boots hung out at the end. They carried him covered out the door.

Outside there were too many of them for the snow crust to support.

"Slide him," said someone who had already sunken up to his knees.

"He'll catch cold."

"He'll catch worse if we don't."

They began to slide Mr. Coulter through the darkness. The man with the lead rope watched for trees. Ahead the revolving red light on the roof of the converted bread truck lit the snow. It was like an airport beacon. Hilda walked behind the men with her mother who was smoking again.

Mory stayed in the boathouse. He looked around at the debris. He saw his mother's guitar on the floor where she had dropped it. He walked over and turned off the amplifier and watched the red light die on the controls. When he went to check the phonograph, he found his grandfather's teeth on the couch. He thought the teeth seemed to watch him come. They were dry and very white. When he put them in his pants pocket they pinched his leg and for a second he thought they might be moving. Then he thought the stuffed animals were moving, too. He shook his head. But everything was really watching him when he put on his parka. And he was thinking things which weren't true.

He stopped at the door and surveyed the damage once more. He knew there was more than this.

Then Mory turned out the lights and stepped into the falling snow.

Fourteen | Mory reached the laundry and dropped over onto the access road. Tired snow swallowed his sneakers and a wind from the hill drove the fresh small dry flakes at his face. He saw light in the open kitchen door. It made a triangular yellow rug on the boardwalk. All vehicles were gone or put away except for Roger's maroon Chevy which looked white. The falling snow did not bother Mory. It was silver.

When he neared the grand old beech tree which Fred wanted to cut down to give the garden more sun, Mory heard his mother. She was speaking excitedly but the boy could not hear what she was saying. Then he heard Fred yelling at her. He could not see either of them. He saw only Suzanne. His sister was sitting in the doorway under the telephone on one of the extra chairs. Then she began yelling too.

Mory stepped behind the tree to listen but he could not make out what any of them were saying. He walked closer, up to the garage corner. He felt slightly guilty, like a trespasser, but he stayed put there.

"None of you should drink never," Fred yelled. "I told

you that. If I'd have been smart, I'd of never had this party. I knew it would be ruined. You had to wreck it, like everything else."

"It wasn't spoiled," Hilda said, almost pleading. "It was nice."

"Nice? Is that what you call it? Your father drunk on his ass."

"It was his heart gave way," Hilda said.

"Bullshit, heart. It was his head."

"It wasn't," the woman said.

"What do you call it? His heart, bullshit. His head was ninety proof. Be in the paper by morning. The boss'll hear too. Then I got to explain to him. Can't you never do nothing right?"

"He looked so miserable," Hilda said. Her voice was saturated. "I want to go see him."

"Will you shut up for once?" Fred yelled. "Drink that coffee like I told you."

"No," said Hilda. She dragged out the simple word almost affirmatively.

"Well, you can't go to no hospital tonight."

Hilda was still very drunk.

"I just want to see him," she said.

"Will you go to bed, Hilda, and worry about the old buzzard in the morning? For Christsakes, after all I done for you, you got to go get stinking drunk. You and your worthless family. None of them is ever coming back here, as long as I got anything to say about it. They had their last of my whiskey."

"Fred," Hilda said, "please."

But Fred wasn't listening to her.

"You know what you were when I met you? Remember? Who dragged your ass out of them bars? Who give you a home and clothes to wear? And your kids, too? Who got them kids out of more trouble than I care to remember? It sure as shit wasn't your old man."

"He's so nicer than you are," Hilda interrupted. "And the way he fell on the floor. Like nobody cared."

"Yeah, well, nobody did. And it ain't the first time. I told him not to drink when he come here. Like talking to a chainsaw. Like filling it up too. And that mother of yours. Drunk as an old bat. Drunker than you are now. She ain't never coming here again. I thought women were ladies when they got over seventy. The whole lot of you, all drunk. I never seen such a bunch of worthless freeloading drunken Indians in my whole life."

"Don't you never call my mother worthless. Don't you never treat her like that. She's worth fifty of yours." Hilda had found an unbroken string of words somewhere.

"Don't you never tell me what I don't say or do," Fred said.

Hilda began crying.

Roger's voice came calmly through the snow to Mory.

"Why don't you shut up and drag your sorry old ass to bed, Fred?"

"Yeah, and you," Fred said turning to Roger. "What did you ever do? Except playing with your balls? Freeloader Freddie himself. The best part of you ran down your father's leg. For two cents I'd throw you and your goddamn cigarettes out of here and let you pitch a tent. I hope you burn up."

"Piss off," Roger said calmly.

"Yeah, piss off, huh? Is that the way you talk in front of your mother? You ain't never showed her no respect anyway. Piss off, huh? Piss off. You better apologize, or."

"Or what?"

"Or I'll beat the shit out of you right in this room."

"Don't you touch him," Suzanne yelled.

"Don't you open your mouth either, you little bitch. There's plenty of things he don't know about you. Remember? There's things you ain't never discussed with him, I bet."

"Like what?" Roger asked.

"Like you really want to know? You want to know what you married? You don't know the half of it. Ask anyone. Ask her brothers. Look at her. Look at them eyes."

They couldn't help themselves. They had to look at Suzanne's eyes. And her eyes were tired, very tired, sad, and worn out.

"Watch yourself," Roger warned. He was being surprisingly reasonable.

"Ask her. Go ahead. Ask her yourself. Ask her how she used to drop her pants for every little thug in town."

"Look, Fred."

"Ask her. Go on. See, you won't. Afraid you might learn something? Afraid you might not slide between them legs so easy if you know what's been in there?"

"Look, Fred, why don't you just go to bed?"

"Who with?" Fred asked stupidly and he laughed at what he had said. There was a brief ceasefire, as if they might sweep the dead words out the door.

"So you don't believe me, Mr. Ithaca? Look at her. She can't even look at you. See? She's fucked out. That's why. And I bet you were too dumb to notice the first time."

"You say one more word about her," Roger said calmly, "and you're through talking for a week."

"The hell with all of you," Fred said, but he came back at Roger. "Listen, buster, you're not too big that the police can't handle you. You want me to call them. Right now?"

"I don't give a rat's ass who you call," Roger said.

"Fred," Hilda said.

But Fred wouldn't hear his wife any more. Now

Suzanne was crying into her hands. It was as though the caretaker had raped her roughly and nothing else mattered.

"Shut your goddamn bawling mouths," Fred said. He was livid and they could see the veins in his neck. "Go ahead and cry, you thieving, whoring little bitch. You think we didn't know all about you? All them nights we had to come pick you up. You think we didn't know? Your mother knew. She washed out your underpants more than once. God knows what else. Even Weaver knew. Yeah, even he knew. And you acting so goddamn cherry around him all the time. And getting favors. Shit, you were the easiest lay in town. I heard them talk."

Then Roger said, "Why, Freddie, you're just a filthy fucking old man." The talk had gone so far that Roger was smiling. "Don't listen to him, Suze. He don't know what he's saying. He's crazy."

"Now I'm crazy," Fred said as though it were possible.

For what seemed a long time Mory stood outside listening to his sister crying. He knew his mother was too drunk to help her.

Fred went on. "Worthless. That's what you all are. A bunch of worthless ungrateful tramps. Like niggers. After all I done for you that's what I get. A bunch of drunken coons who ain't got one manner between them. I should have known better. Always using me all the time. You think I didn't know it? I knew it. All of you. Joe Ben and John and them goddamn whore wives of theirs."

Mory began walking toward the house. He was not sure of what he would say or do but he wanted everybody to stop cold.

"None of you is any good. When I think of the times I tried to help you. Cheating behind my back. And what do I get? Shit."

Mory could not feel the snow where it struck him. He

was thinking he did not want to slip, not now. He'd had enough.

"You through?" Roger asked.

"I'm through with you, bub. I'm through when I want to be through. This is my house you're using and I'm through with all of you. Every goddamn son of a bitching freeloading lasting goddamn one of you. I wish I'd never seen the filth of you. Cleaned you up and gave you manners and what do I get?"

"Shit," said Roger.

Mory stomped his feet at the door. Nobody spoke. He stopped next to Suzanne.

His mother was slumped in a chair near the counter. A full cup of black cold coffee shook on the table in front of her. She had her elbows on the table and the flesh was loose on her forearms. There were furrows in her face powder where the tears had run, revealing the little pockmarks in her skin. Fred was standing in the corner between the sink and stove. He had taken off his shirt and his undershirt sleeves were stuck up under his armpits. His hands were clenched in fists at his sides and his fly zipper was halfway open so the pattern on his underpants showed. Roger leaned against the living room doorway. He was using the floor for an ashtray and looking down where the tracked snow had melted and discolored the tile. He rubbed his left sideburn with his free hand. Suzanne was crying in long agonized sobs.

"Well, here's Mr. Clean," Fred said, seeing Mory. "Where you think you're going?"

"Don't talk to him," Suzanne managed to say.

"See?" said Fred to all and nobody in particular.

"To bed," Mory said, but he had not moved past his sister.

"At least you ain't going to get fucked," Fred said. "For all I know, you're going to."

"Leave him alone," Roger said, "and shut your filthy goddamn mouth."

"What do I know?" Fred asked softly. He could have been calling unseen spirits. "What do I ever know about any of you? I never should have gotten myself into this mess. I never thought." He paused and then went on speaking very softly. "I really never thought I'd have got mixed up with a batch of pimps and whores. People used to tell me things but I wouldn't listen. Poor Fred, they'd say, he's so lonesome. Yeah, well, maybe I was. But I ain't going to be no more. No more never."

Mory walked around his sister and the table. When he reached Fred and stood up to him, he could see the gray hairs sprouting over the neck of the caretaker's undershirt. He saw the folds of loose neck skin. Briefly he was fascinated.

"What do you want?" the caretaker asked, his voice rising again. He seemed ready to step back from the boy. "Well don't just stand there looking at me like a burnt strip of bacon."

Slowly Mory raised his eyes until they met Fred's. He could see how dark his stepfather's eyes were and he hated them first, then all of the caretaker.

"Come on, take your piece of Fred," the old man said. "Everybody else has."

"Fred," Mory said wearily. "Tonight you're so disgusting."

Fred's left hand caught the boy's head broadside. The caretaker had plenty of strength and his hand, open and swung in an arc, had partly lifted the boy onto the kitchen table before the smack was heard.

Mory felt the force shake him and heard Suzanne scream but then his mother was on her feet to protect him.

"Don't you touch him never," Hilda yelled. "You hurt him enough already. I'll kill you if you do again."

Her vehemence surprised Fred and he stepped back to watch her prop up the boy. If she had come for him, he could not have stepped back any farther. But Hilda was pulling Mory toward the open door.

"Where the fuck you think you're going?" Fred asked. He sounded desperate.

"Home," Hilda said, stopping.

"Home? You ain't got no home. This here's your home. Or was."

"Was my home," Hilda said, starting up and tugging Mory. "We're going home."

It made sense.

Mory didn't know where they were going and he wasn't crying. His head stung from the slap and he had to close his eyes to stop the stars. He did not open his eyes until he felt the snow soft on his face. The snow was still silver to him and he recognized it like a friend as he caught up with his mother, dragging him.

They went quickly around the driveway toward the road. When one of them slipped, the other hung on. They were using each other blindly, like two convicts escaping in handcuffs. Under the trees it was very dark and the wind drove snow into their faces. Their hands were bare.

Hilda stopped at the road to look both ways as if there could be traffic. Then she turned right toward town and started walking slowly. It was as though they were beginning a journey and needed to conserve everything. Neither of them looked into the house when they passed. The plows had been along within the hour and the road was slick. They walked struggling.

Soon Mory heard his mother breathing hard. As long as they were moving, he knew they wouldn't feel the cold. He heard his heart and his head throbbed badly but he did not want to stop in the dark.

When they reached the first bend, they were barely

walking. On the right was a driveway to another camp and they stepped over the plowed bank off the road and stopped.

Hilda just sighed.

"Where we going?" Mory asked.

"I don't know yet," his mother said. She sat down in the snow and dragged him down with her. Instantly their legs were cold.

"I really just don't know anymore," Hilda said. She was breathing the fresh cold air in gulps. "I never seen him like that before."

"He didn't know what he was saying," Mory said.

"He knew. He couldn't hold himself no more. He knew what he's been thinking for a long time, Mory."

"He never said it before."

"He said it now, didn't he?" She hugged the boy until it hurt. "How much of it you hear?"

"What can we do now?" he asked.

"I got to think," his mother said, but she dropped her head and began crying again. "I just got to think. I never had to think this much. I can't do us no good here. But I got to make everything all right."

"Maybe he's better now," Mory said. "He's been this bad before. Maybe we can go back."

Suddenly his mother lay back in the driveway and stretched herself out flat like a dead bear. It was startling how quickly the snow covered her hair.

"I don't want to go back. I don't want you to go back neither." She was crying old tears.

"Don't cry," he said. "We can't stay here. We'd freeze by morning."

"Yeah," Hilda said, like it was a solution. "We'll freeze, Mory. You and me'll freeze. Nobody knows. Anything will be better."

Then Mory saw lights on the road and he said, "I don't want to freeze, Mom. Someone's coming."

Hilda sat up.

The car came slowly through the snow.

"He's looking for us," Hilda said. She was still too drunk to sound scared.

"He'll find us," Mory said. "He can track us here." The boy didn't think he was afraid.

"We got to go," Hilda said. She tried to stand up but she couldn't.

The car stopped at the driveway and they heard the windshield wipers slap above the engine. They stayed huddled together as the door opened.

"Come on," Roger said. "Get in. I'll take you home. The old fucker's abed now."

Fifteen | Late at night Mory was honest. He was isolated and there was no interference. He could lie in his bed listening to sounds and identifying them. He was alone but never lonely and he could think honestly.

Now he heard the snow brush the window and the wind shirking off the hill. The storm was good to hear and there was nothing else. The wind was a force the boy understood and maybe loved, something powerful which could not touch him here alone. If this force ever hurt him, it would be hurting everyone else. Then he would not be alone.

He thought he heard his mother speak to Fred. Probably they were trying to talk softly because the walls of the house were thin. The sound he heard was just a mumble. He heard Fred at the toilet and then a bed creaking as his stepfather lay down. His mother seemed to still be speaking but Mory did not try to hear her. He remembered how she had held him tightly in the snow and how he had pulled away from her. Then he heard his mother go into the bathroom and vomit, a strong rush of herself followed by a splash and gulps dying into choked coughs. In his mind he saw Hilda's insides, their browness in the bowl, bits of sour stew and too much vodka mixed. He heard it all flushed away and he forgot it all immediately.

Under the door he saw a light turned on in the hallway and he heard his mother's tired padded feet. He did not want to see her again so he rolled over toward the window where he could pretend to sleep. His window was barely open but the new part of the pillow felt cold beneath his temple where Fred had slapped him. He did not mind the slap anymore and he kept his eyes open. His mother passed the door and soon the light was gone. He knew she would be sleeping on the couch.

At first he listened to the old house struggle to avoid the weather. He was thinking of John and Sara. He was glad they had not stayed for the party. John would have acted differently than Roger. Roger was nearly always cool when he should have been hot. John would have gotten very hot. Mory could remember at least three times that evening when John would have boiled and he knew his brother would have struck their stepfather each time. John had hit Fred before, as hard as he could. One time John had been killing the caretaker until Hilda broke it up with her crying. Somehow they had gotten over that crush and come together again as a family. But it had taken an unpleasant time. John had gone to live in town and they had not seen him for two weeks. When he came back Fred said he had forgotten the incident but Mory knew he had never forgiven his brother. Since then Fred was scared of John. He knew only too well how John had served bad time in the reformatory and then volunteered for infantry reconnaissance to get free. And John came back stronger. He always came back from everything he did. But although John could be very bad, Mory knew his brother was good inside, better, at least, than most. It was as though at times John needed to be the opposite of himself.

Then Mory remembered how after his accident when he had lain in bed and Hilda had changed his sheets daily to avoid infection, John had come to see him with a huge rainbow trout. It was certainly larger than any laker Fred had taken trolling that year. Fred and Hilda had warned John not to bring the dripping fish into the boy's room but he had walked right in and let Mory feel the fish, still wet and firm, its last colors seeming to fade into the bed with the water from the bucket. That fish had been good for Mory and made him want to get well. He had pleaded with John to reveal where he caught it but John wouldn't tell right away. Later he told his younger brother he would show him when he was well. He said Mory would have to try to beat him with his own fish. It was a simply fantastic fish and Mory had then pleaded with John to have it mounted. John had just shook his head and laughed as he gave the fish to Hilda who baked it for their supper. That rainbow had tasted tough but fantastic.

John was good but Sara was the best. She was Mory's brother's wife and his niece's mother and his best friend but the boy knew he loved her. He couldn't help it. He had never knowingly loved anybody but he knew he loved Sara completely. He didn't want to understand why and he never mentioned this. His love for her was just something warm to be recognized in himself and it was something else he could do nothing about. Mory had been very close to other people and he had done certain things with them but he had never wanted to be near anyone as much as with Sara. Now, remembering her parting invitation, he saw her again in his mind. She was sitting at his feet darkly, and he wanted to be near her very much.

Mory heard a plow beginning to push down the road and he waited. Gradually the headlights framed his window and brightened the full sleeves of snow blown against the panes. He heard the truck's motor roaring against the night and the huge pointed plow scraping snow from the ice ruts. The plow sounded more like a big dozer working gravel. The boy breathed the fresh night air deeply. The noise increased until it filled the little room like a man's growl. Then the lights were gone with the noise down the road. Mory knew the plow would be back and he pulled the Hudson Bay blanket up over his ear as if to prepare for it.

In winter the road had little enough traffic but in summer there were always tourists. Mory would sit out front on the grass near Hilda's rose bushes and watch the tourists driving by. He would see the people point at him. He would read their license plates and wonder what they thought they were doing, crammed inside, whole families of them, in big long cars pulling house trailers or boats easily. And he would wonder what it might be like where they really lived and if they, too, sat on their lawns and watched other tourists, maybe Adirondackers, and then shook their heads, glad not to be going anywhere. Mory had no real desire to see other places yet but he wanted to be able to go when he changed his mind. Usually his curiosity was half asleep unless he forced it. Then he wanted to know everything. Yet he studied the tourists and learned things.

Once Samuel Weaver had a guest in camp who jogged three miles every day regardless of weather. He ran like a rite. He was into his thirties and remarkably fit for a banker who drank. He was not ashamed to wear only shorts and a special pair of striped running shoes. When he discovered how Mory lifted weights and punched the tired speed bag in the garage, he invited the boy to jog with him.

Mory had not wanted to go running with the guest but he went. Tourists passed them constantly and they could not resist somehow jeering the strong man in shorts sweating out yesterday's alcohol and the boy in his old blue Saranac Lake sweatsuit keeping discreetly behind. They called them every unnecessary name, and some worse, and they fed them sand and pure exhaust. One family even turned their car around to have another look at them, as if running on a state highway were extraordinary.

Mory had not felt the tourists. He had felt only his skin slick with sweat under the jersey and the dampness on his legs, and all of himself had felt good and given him a pride in what he was doing with the older man. The run was never a contest and they ran well together.

Then nearing camp another car slowed beside them and a man with a bald, sunburned head had lowered his air-conditioned window and begun to clock them on the speedometer. Mory and the guest were slowing down. They ignored the tourist's reports by looking dead ahead and not responding. The guest had seemed magnificently strong. But a boy in the back seat could not resist rolling down his window and spitting at the guest's bare chest. It was a simple act and there had been laughter from inside the car. The guest waved the boy off with his fist but the youngster spat a second time. Then the guest shook his fist in stride and politely told them all to fuck themselves. It was an equally simple act. It was something Mory could never do but he had loved the simple way there had been no more spitting or discussing after that.

Now he remembered how quickly the tourists had vanished and how the guest had offered him one of Weaver's beers when they got back to camp and how they had both gone swimming in the lake to cool off.

And then on summer nights in nice weather Mory would lie back in the grass and watch shooting stars like the ones he held now always in his bad eye. Sometimes he would dream of grander things and the distance between places, still not knowing. And the wind would die at once, and the day's last batch of biting bugs would rush for his skin, and he would pick himself up and go inside to the television and his family, and they would have the traffic and the Weavers and the bugs and the day's heat to talk about loosely until they went to bed.

All that seemed so very far away to Mory and so did the party and Fred and the road and his mother and the snow and John and Sara.

Sixteen | They slept well into morning. There were no inside sounds to the house but outside the storm advanced strongly, shaking the house as it came. It was like a wounded animal which had not bothered to collect itself before charging. Wind gusted rudely off the hill and shoved the plowed snow onto the highway, forcing tall dunes. The road shrank under the assault. Near the house where there was lots of old snow, the wind pushed the new snow into the trees and up against the windows until the bottom panes were coated. Beneath the bay window Hilda's flower box had vanished and her bird feeding stations nailed onto the trees were threatened. All the time more snow fell in howling swirls and landed heavily. That was outside where the new day was like a rugged unfinished painting.

Mory woke first and he did not mind the storm. He pushed back the covers slowly as if rediscovering himself. His room was very cold and he had to poke out snow with his fingers to close the window. When he dressed hurriedly he found his grandfather's teeth. They were chilly and they clicked loudly when he yanked them from his pocket.

The hall was quiet and gray. Jimmy was awake, staring disdainfully at his empty milk saucer on the kitchen floor. Hilda sprawled on the couch in the living room. Her blanket was pulled up to her chin so her knobby ankles and feet were exposed. Her soles were dirty. Without her glasses, she looked dead.

There was no door to close to the living room so Mory tried to be quiet as he built the coffee. Every sound he made seemed doubly loud. He dumped the old grounds, refueled the basket, filled the pot with water, and set the works on the stove. He opened the burner all the way and the gas flame caught with a pop. Jimmy came over and brushed by his leg importantly.

Mory was not hungry yet so he sat at the table and let the cat jump onto his lap. The kitchen was quiet and the cat was soft. When he stroked Jimmy, the cat purred and some gray hairs came loose in the boy's hand. Mory enjoyed having the cat until the percolator was bubbling brown in the bulb. When he stood up to lower the heat, he smelled the finishing coffee richly and he thought it was a grand smell to have in the morning.

Mory was careful with the icebox door as he got Jimmy's milk and he was careful not to spill when he filled the saucer. He watched how the cat drank innocently, first slowly, then with some gentle noise.

The wall clock reached eight-thirty and ran on.

Mory got out the tube of pork sausage and a can of unsweetened orange juice which he shook before opening. The juice did not seem sour when he drank two full glasses to get himself going. Then the coffee was made enough and he poured a cup, using milk and too much sugar when he fixed it. The coffee was too sweet so he wasted it in the sink and started over. He was being very quiet and behaving and hearing only himself and he was beginning to function. He got out the bread and a carton of eggs and set them near the sink. When he sliced the sausage through the wrapper, he moved the coffee pot off the flame and replaced it with an iron skillet. The pan met the burner loudly and he winced. He removed the wrappers from the sausage and began to mold the patties with his hands. The sausage withdrew slightly under his grip and it sizzled sharply as it hit the hot pan. Then Mory's hands were greasy and he had to wipe them with a dry paper towel before he did anything else. The smells were getting good now and he tried his coffee again, smelling it more than tasting, to bring himself around fully. Jimmy lay down near the stove, full and needing a share of the warmth. Mory could hear the wind but it did not bother him and he did not look for it. He flipped the sausages casually with a long barbecue spatula and then he broke five eggs into a Pyrex bowl and added a measure of milk. The blend stirred gooey and right, like yellow saliva. It would not separate with the spoon whipping it. If it did, it could be brought back.

Mory was busy now and he did not hear Hilda getting up. He did not notice her in the doorway until she spoke. Her feet were bare and she wore the blanket over her slumping shoulders, pulled in at the waist, the way an Indian would.

"What you doing, Mory?" she asked with the sleep in her eyes.

"Cooking something," the boy said.

His mother yawned widely. "What you cooking?" Her voice was barely awake.

"Sausage," he said.

"Was it still good?"

Hilda tried to rub her eyes without losing the blanket. Briefly the boy saw her breasts largely.

"It smells good."

"It's been there a long time. I was going to give it to the cat."

"We'll give it to him if it don't taste good. I gave him some milk."

"What's in that bowl there?"

"Egg."

"What kind of egg?"

"I'm going to whip up some French toast."

"You're a good boy, Mory," his mother said. She seemed almost dazed. "You're the best I got."

"Quit it," Mory said, pressing the grease from the sausage with the spatula. He was not bothering with her or what she was saying. She could be ugly in the morning.

Hilda stayed in the doorway.

Finally she picked up her head and asked, "How'd you sleep?"

"Easy," he said.

"I didn't even know I was sleeping," his mother said. "I didn't even know if I could sleep after what happened. But I slept on the couch."

"That was yesterday," Mory said and he reached for a plate and covered it with a paper towel to drain the sausage.

"It's still the same snow," Hilda said.

"You going to eat?" Mory asked.

"I got to get my slippers. My feet are cold as icebergs."

The woman looked at her feet and they held a fascination for her for about a minute.

"Go get them."

"I shouldn't wake up Fred."

"Why not?"

"He was in that bad mood last night. I don't know what he's like today. He don't get like that much, Mory. You know that. He wasn't hisself. I think he's worried. I better not bother him."

Mory was pouring off most of the grease from the frying pan. He stirred the egg again and plunked a piece of bread into the blend. The bread floated.

"I wonder how he'll be today," Hilda said.

"Why don't you go find out?"

"Maybe I shouldn't wake him, Mory. Where's Suzanne and Roger?"

Mory flipped the bread with a fork to soak up both sides.

"Still sleeping."

"I wonder what they're thinking."

"Who?"

His mother smiled. "All of them. But I was thinking of Suze and him in particular. They come all this way and had to get into the fight. I wish it could have been just our fight. Didn't have to include them all. Seems like they won't want to come no more."

He saw she was sad.

"They'll come," he said, forking the bread into the pan so it sizzled. The batter formed quickly in pale yellow drops around the crust.

"Seems like everything we do turns out wrong," Hilda said. "And we can't do nothing about it neither. We try to make a nice party and we try to be a family together but nothing works right. Nothing has ever worked, Mory. Do you know that?" Her voice had risen but it fell again as she added, "Nothing has ever worked for us ever."

Mory didn't know what to make of her. He wished she would leave him alone and go get dressed. He turned the toast brown side up and he dropped another piece of bread into the batter.

"This stove works," he said.

"I wish I did," Hilda said. "I don't feel too good yet. That French toast don't even make me hungry."

"Go get your shoes," Mory said. "Wake them all up and tell them it's here. They can eat if they want. Then come on back and have coffee. You'll feel better."

"Maybe I should," Hilda said. "You're a good boy, Mory. Don't let nobody tell you you're not."

He saw her troop down the hall, strangely soft on her big soiled feet. He thought she would tell him she loved him if she could.

When the two pieces of toast were done, Mory found the syrup bottle in the cupboard and wrapped paper towel around it to hide the stickiness. Then he fixed himself a plate and sat down to eat alone.

By now he was hungry.

Seventeen | The others came along slowly. Hilda was first but she only took coffee and her hands shook as she set the cup on the table. Next came Suzanne who fried more toast for Roger and herself. Roger had to put out a cigarette to eat. He put what was left of it into his pocket to smoke later.

Mory had finished when Fred arrived. The caretaker was wearing socks and an undershirt and he had not washed or shaved. He sat down and began to clean his glasses.

Hilda fixed his breakfast. She poured his coffee and stirred it white with milk and sugar, the way he always drank it. When she set Fred's plate in front of him, they were all watching the caretaker.

"French toast," Fred said, reaching for the margarine. "I wonder if they really eat this in France."

The caretaker spread margarine smoothly onto the stack of toast. He squinted and lifted each piece as if it were necessary to inspect his breakfast. He took his time.

"Syrup, please."

Roger passed the open bottle.

"Hell of a storm."

They all turned toward the window but the wind was blowing so hard they couldn't see through the panes.

"This is the big one," Fred said, carving everything on his plate into little pieces. "I knew we'd get one more. I just knew it."

When the caretaker finally began eating, he made his own special noises. Those who still had something left to eat ate silently. Hilda sat down again, still with her first cup of coffee.

"I hate to see that boathouse," Fred said. "I hate to even think about it."

Jimmy was licking his paws in the corner.

"Let's see. We're going to have to go over there first. Roger, you and Suzanne can help. The boss could surprise us. Then I got to see about that truck. Probably pretty deep to plow already. If I'd of been able to work yesterday, we'd of been all right. Don't know about it now though. Got to see."

Fred moistened every bite of his food with coffee, so he could swallow. He seemed to be talking through the food. Really he was talking to himself.

"We may not be able to get you to town, Ma. We'll sure try. Is the phones working? You could call first and see if there's any use going."

The caretaker's words hung unanswered but he kept talking through the silences he made.

"If I can get us to the road, we can make it to the hospital. That don't bother me so much as if they can get back in there with the oil. I got to keep that road open. I knew I should have called them and had them bring the truck out here last week. But I didn't think of it. I should have known about this storm. I was just too busy."

Now Fred realized he was talking to himself and he stopped eating,

"Roger, you and Suzanne clean up that boathouse enough to make it look good. I can get to the truck. I don't want Ma out in this weather. She's already sick and she had enough last night."

Roger lit his half cigarette.

Fred nodded, like a king who knew everything. Then he finished his breakfast and motioned for Hilda to remove his plate. She fixed him more coffee without asking. Out of habit Fred reached for a cigarette but there weren't even pockets to his T-shirt. The gesture looked ridiculous and he knew it.

"Thanks, Ma," he said when Hilda brought the coffee. "That was good. That was what I needed. What's the matter, ain't anybody talking here?"

"Mory thought to make the French toast," Hilda said quickly. She was sitting down again.

"Mory's the only smart one of us here," Fred said definitely. "Ain't that right, Mory?"

"Mory was first up," Hilda said, as though to her it was an honor.

"Mory's the only one who ain't feeling no pain," Fred said and he grinned around his teeth stupidly. "I sure don't know what happened last night. I guess I got myself a little high. I might have done some things."

"You were just knee-walking, commode-hugging drunk, Fred." Roger said. "You did lots of strange things." He blew a trail of smoke at the ceiling which they could all follow.

"Yeah, well, I wasn't the only one," Fred said. "But you got to blow off a little steam now and then. Cooped up like this. Everybody does it."

"You could have pulled a train," Roger said. "You must be plumb steamed out." Roger might have gone on but Suzanne put her hand on his knee under the table. He looked pleased with himself as he smoked.

"I got sick," Hilda announced to change the subject. "I must have drank too much."

"Maybe you just ate too much," Fred said. "You'd been sick anyway, Ma. We shouldn't have had that party until you was well. I told you that. But it's done now. And we got a hell of a mess to clean up."

"No," Roger said slowly. "You do, Fred. We're leaving."

Fred gave Roger his first dirty look of the day.

"So you're just going to leave, huh? Well, I'd just like to see you leave. I bet you can't go nowhere even if you could. I bet you can't even move out of the driveway. Not until I get the truck fixed. I bet you're stuck here, bub, and I bet you better start acting like it."

"I bet I can," Roger said, taunting him. He smoked his second cigarette remarkably smoothly, as though it were pure lasting gold. He was ready for anything the caretaker might say.

But Fred wasn't arguing. He slapped his hands on the table and said, "Shit, I give up." He did look too tired to move.

Suzanne had not spoken. Now she stood up and began to stack the dishes on the table. She seemed prettier in the morning, as though all the abuse she had taken the night before had helped her. Fred just stared at her, like he owned her, and was considering the best price she'd bring. Hilda didn't try to help her and Mory didn't have to. It was as though Suzanne were the only one capable of moving accurately and even her scant routine movements became unusual, like a performance. She stacked the dishes loudly and then, when she realized she was being watched, she sat down again, as if uncertain how to proceed.

"Well," Fred said to nobody in particular.

"Well," said Roger mimicking him.

"Well, what?"

"Well, shit," Roger said.

Mory leaned way back in the chair and reached into his pants pocket.

"Here," the boy said, "are grandfather's teeth."

Eighteen | Mory switched the radio to WNBZ. After months in the lounge chair he knew what each announcer would say over the local radio station. He knew their choicest expressions and favorite records. Even when there was a substitute announcer Mory knew what he would say and practically how he would say it. Any new man had probably worked at the station previously, quit to take another job, failed at that, and then come back. That was how small the town was.

Mory sat in his chair listening to the announcements. There were closings of schools and facilities and cancellations of civic and recreational organizations. Then he heard about driving conditions. He heard about roads between Saranac Lake and Lake Placid and Tupper Lake and Bloomingdale and Malone. He heard the state police had already issued a bulletin from their substation in Ray Brook advising people to stay home. Ski areas were still open but their directors were uncertain about how long lifts could be kept moving. The various directors bragged about snow conditions at Whiteface, Big Tupper, Scott's Cobble, and even Mt. Pisgah. There was more. There would be a camping and outdoor show at the Olympic Arena in Lake Placid on Saturday and Sunday. One of Monday night's duplicate bridge scores had been announced incorrectly and the correction was made. The week's bowling scores were brought up to date. The Strawberry Garden Club would not meet again until May because the president had gone to

Florida. Three students from the new community college in Saranac Lake were arrested on the street Wednesday night and charged with possession of a dangerous drug. A town waterpipe had burst somewhere. Someone had ridden a snowmobile into a tree and suffered lacerations of the arms, neck, head, and face. Someone else had died and would be buried in the spring. The body was available for viewing until Saturday when a High Requiem Mass would be held. Mr. Harry Rebel Coulter had been taken to the Saranac Lake General Hospital by the Saranac Lake Rescue Squad after suffering a seizure at a camp on the Upper Lake. Two men had responded to the call at 10:48 P.M. Down in Albany the governor had taken time off to praise the work done by his specially appointed Temporary Study Commission for the Future of the Adirondacks. Up in Plattsburg several real estate moguls had verbally assaulted the same commission. Mohawk Airlines continued to be grounded by a pilots strike caused by a dispute over time, wages, and benefits. The airline's management hoped to have their aircraft flying a limited schedule by spring unless they merged. The Adirondack Airport in Lake Clear was closed to all traffic except emergencies. The local high school sports scores were incomplete. The bobsled run near Lake Placid would probably not reopen next year because of state budgetary problems but a number of sliding enthusiasts were trying to save it for the Olympic Games to be held in Denver in 1976. The Games Committee did not contemplate building a run in Colorado. Writing letters about this disaster to the local economy was encouraged. Anyone could write. A deer had been killed by wild dogs near Corey's and someone in Tupper Lake was eighty-four years old today. Otherwise everything was normal except for the storm.

Mory heard how the storm had originated in the southern plains states and gone east to Missouri and turned north in West Virginia and Pennsylvania where it met the fringes of a frigid arctic air mass blowing down from Canada. The two fronts had locked horns over the southern frontier of western New York and then moved slowly northeast during the night until they stalled over the Adirondacks. Rochester, Syracuse, and Buffalo had declared states of snow emergency. Motorists throughout the western portion of the state were advised not to drive. The storm, probably the worst of the year, would be in the Tri-Lakes area at least forty-eight hours before moving out toward Nova Scotia. Around Catyville and Chazy the winds had reached fifty miles per hour and snow drifts were already estimated at fifteen to twenty feet in places. Today was March 5.

Mory heard all this news from his lounger and none of it mattered. If he hadn't been seeing the storm through the window, it could have been happening in Meeteetse, Wyoming.

When Suzanne's baby woke, she made oatmeal for the child and brought her into the living room. The little girl was already active and her mother had to hold her. No lights were on in the sitting room.

"You O.K.?" Mory asked his sister. "You haven't said much. I thought maybe you was worried."

"I'm O.K.," Suzanne said, fixing the child's jumper suit. "I just feel like I've been stretched way out of shape by what he said. But I'm O.K."

"You held up good," Mory said. He turned down the volume of the radio which now played music he recognized.

"I didn't feel like arguing with him," his sister said. "I've seen him bad before like that and it ain't worth it."

"He really put some words on you."

"I know," Suzanne said. She shrugged. "Who cares? So what?"

"It was a bitch," Mory said.

"Well, I can leave, can't I? I ain't like you anymore, Mory. I don't have to put up with it."

"He pretty much lets me alone."

"Well, he ought to. After what he did to you. You should have sued him."

"For what?"

"I don't know," she said, shrugging again. She was talking to Mory but concentrating on the squirming child. "Fred ain't worth much."

"Maybe I could have taken him for a head of lettuce."

Mory was trying to cheer her up.

"It'd be poison," she said. "Anything he touches is poison. He's like a germ. A filthy goddamn germ."

"Then I'm infected," Mory said. "Because he sure touched me last night."

"I didn't mean that, Mory. He used to hit me plenty. He tried some other things, too. Some of the things he said were just as bad."

"Maybe you shouldn't come around for a while, Suze. He don't seem right anymore when there's company."

"Don't worry. We won't. If we ever get out of here."

"You really think you'll try today? The roads sound bad."

"Do they?" she said shrugging. "What's the difference? What's worse than this?"

Mory nodded.

"Rog thinks we'll make it. He's going to put chains on the car. He drives good and he don't mind weather. That's the best thing he does is drive."

She laughed for a second and her smile was nice.

"He said we could get out. He said we'd walk if we had to."

"You better take a blanket for the baby."

"I got one. I ain't taking nothing out of here and I ain't bringing nothing back. I ain't coming back."

"You got to come back, Suze. Wait until good weather though. Come back in May."

"Why?" she asked.

"We can do some fishing."

"I can fish at home."

"Besides," Mory said slowly, "you still got your mother here."

"Who? She can't be no mother if she's husband to him. She's a goddamn slave, Mory, like in the movies. You seen it."

"He's just too old," Mory said. Then he saw Fred at the doorway with Hilda.

Mory didn't know what they'd heard as he watched them enter the room. Fred walked funny because he was trying to zip up the front of his insulated coveralls. They were the sort snowmobilers use, blue and quilted, with red racing stripes around the sleeves. Zipped up to his neck, Fred resembled a prepared child. Hilda wore her ski clothes. She carried Fred's gloves, his hat, and his rubber and canvas pacs. He had already put on the felt liners and he sat down to buckle on the outer boots. His glasses were steaming.

"Going to be colder than a boar's ass in a well hole," he said, bending way over and showing his bald spot.

"Whyn't you just call someone to come and plow for you?" Hilda asked pleasantly.

"Yeah, and what do you think the boss would say about that?"

"You done it for shoveling the roofs, Pa. Mr. Weaver told you to get all the help you needed."

"Yeah, he did tell me that but he also told me to keep the bills down. Remember? Him and all his money."

The caretaker had trouble with the last buckle. Finally it caught and he sat up. He was perspiring.

Hilda handed him the gloves and the red plastic cap with the fake fur ear muffs.

When Fred stood up to finish dressing, he was breathing heavily. When he went toward the door, his gait was exaggerated, like an astronaut boarding the command module.

"I hope he don't catch cold," Hilda said. "Should I fix you some coffee?"

Neither of her children wanted coffee so Hilda went over and switched on the television. The quiz program was not one of her favorites and she did not correct the color imbalance.

"Will you really try to leave today, Suzanne?" Hilda asked. She was sitting on the couch at some distance from her daughter. She kept one eye on the TV screen.

"We're leaving," Suzanne said, "as soon as we can."

"I wish you wouldn't go in this weather. It's not safe. Is Roger a good driver?"

"You know what kind of driver he is, Mother."

"I know, but I worry."

"If we get out of here, you don't have to worry."

"I'm sorry, Suzanne, about last night. I hope you're not leaving because of that. Fred says things he don't mean. You're a big girl now."

"Fred says things he don't know. He never knows what he's saying. Don't think I don't know about him. I think he's the ugliest man I ever saw."

"He don't mean to be," Hilda said. "I'm sorry he hurt you."

"He didn't hurt me. It's Mory he hurt."

Hilda glanced at her son.

"I know," she said forlornly. "And Mory don't know how to hurt nobody. I know that."

Roger came into the room. He was wearing his ski

parka with a sweater underneath and he had combed his hair.

"You going out to help Fred?" Hilda asked. "He needs help, Roger."

"He can help himself," Roger said. "I'm going to put the chains on."

"Do you want coffee?"

"Maybe after I get back."

"All right," Hilda said as Roger also went out.

Nineteen | The morning began to slip by unimportantly. The television showed Hilda one program after another. Suzanne left the living room frequently and came back nervously. Mory thumbed the fishing catalogues and some of the old newspapers Martin Findle had brought. When his eyes tired he watched television. He saw two divorces reenacted, a dating game with a minor Hollywood starlet for the grand prize, and countless dollars, appliances, furnishings, and recreational items being given away to anxious housewives. Then he saw a news special about the disastrous effects of an earthquake in southern California. When there were none of these, the screen showed him a million advertized products to contemplate owning. Outside the storm came on relentlessly and now the wind qualified it for a blizzard and the road plows were only gray ghosts beyond the window. What they did was not evident one minute after they had passed.

Roger was first to return. He said the chains were on and he told Suzanne they were leaving. He was cold.

"You'll stay for lunch," Hilda said. She was absorbed with television so her words were not a question.

"We'll eat on the way if we feel like it," Roger said. "Maybe Tupper. Maybe Cranberry Lake. After that we won't stop."

"Why don't you just stay? I'll fix you some soup and a sandwich. You can take it with you."

They would have left right then if Suzanne had not looked out the window. All she saw was white.

Slowly she said, "We could stay for a while."

"We're leaving," Roger said roughly. "The longer we stay, the worse it gets."

"Just for lunch," Hilda said. "That won't be so bad."

"Might as well warm up, Rog," Mory said.

They agreed to stay.

When Fred came in, his hands were blue, swollen and oily. He was blowing on them loudly and they must have hurt. Hilda stood up to greet him. She looked concerned.

"Did you fix it?"

"Shit, I can't do nothing with that plow," Fred said. "I guess I'm going to have to get some help." He aimed his disgust at Roger.

"That's a shame," Roger said. "You better get somebody who can do something. Somebody who knows something."

"The best thing I could do for that truck is to drive it onto the middle of the lake and let it sink when the ice goes out."

Roger grinned at the old man. "Be pretty hard to explain that one to your boss."

"Yeah, well, just let me worry about that one, bub. At least I got a boss."

"Don't worry," Roger said, grinning, "I'll do that."

The caretaker began loosening his coveralls zipper carefully, as if his ribs might fall out. When Fred removed his glasses to dry them, his eyes were bleary from the cold. His nose was red and he stumbled as he sat down.

"Why don't you lay down for a while," Hilda said. "Take a nap. I'll call you when your lunch is ready. You worked too hard, Pa."

"Yeah, and I didn't get nothing done I wanted," Fred said. "I don't think I could sleep anyway. Too much noise in here."

"We'd be quiet."

"Yeah, but I couldn't rest noway. Too much on my mind."

"Must be tough," Roger said.

"I thought you was leaving."

"We decided to wait until you plowed."

Fred didn't bother with him. He just looked away and shook his head. He picked up an unfinished crossword puzzle, studied it for a second, and set it down. They were all watching him.

Finally the old caretaker said, "Crap, Ma, my back hurts. I shouldn't have tried to do that by myself. I guess I'll go lay down for a little while."

"Why don't you, Fred," Hilda said but she was watching television.

Twenty | After lunch the wind relaxed for a while. They watched the snow fall. It fell thickly but gently without the wind. The hill was stark white and the tree branches looked heavy, like dark veins bent into marble. By now the plows had pushed the snow over the camp mailbox so it was hidden. Along the tennis court fence near the road the snow was two feet from the top. The plows had caused that, too.

Roger had to go outside again to shovel the latest plowed bank from the driveway mouth. When Mory pulled back a thermal curtain to check Roger's progress, all he could see was his head and the shovel blade when it came up. He could not hear Roger swearing.

There was now twelve inches of fresh snow in the driveway. There would have been more had the dirt road not been lined with pine trees which hung somewhat into it. The drive was largely sheltered from sun and snow but it was slippery. The tops of the pines were bent and mostly white.

Roger figured that if he could get a running start from the garage and keep moving through the bend, he would make it out onto the road. Initially he would need all the speed and traction he could get safely. Once onto the road he would tap the brakes and spin the wheel and hope the car would drift around toward Tupper Lake before hitting the snowbank on the other side. The highway was down to one narrow lane and if the drift pointed him toward Saranac Lake, he would probably not be able to turn around until the fish hatchery. But he considered that possibility all right. Getting onto the road was the problem and by now Roger wanted to do that like an obsession. He shoveled away furiously until the wind gusted again and blew a full load onto his back.

Roger left the blue coal shovel in the garage and started his car to warm it for the baby. He scraped the windshield and then he shut the engine off and went into the house.

They were all sitting in the living room waiting for him. Suzanne and the baby were dressed warmly. Their one cracked suitcase stood on the rug near the tape recorder. It was tied with string to keep from bursting.

"So you're going to try it," Fred said. He was down to his undershirt and working a puzzle.

"You set?" Roger asked Suzanne.

"You bet," she said and stood up quickly.

"Let's go."

"Do you really want to?" Hilda asked from the platform rocker. Her question seemed to hold them.

"We got to," Roger said.

"I wish you'd stay tonight."

"Let them go, Ma," Fred said rudely, as if they were selling something he didn't want.

While Suzanne collected the baby's things, Roger went over and shook hands with Mory.

"I hope you make it," Mory said.

"You, too," Roger said smiling. "Good luck, man."

Mory smiled back. "You're going to need a flagger when you hit the road."

"There ain't a whole hell of a lot of traffic. There ain't much going on."

"I'll do it," Hilda said, and she stood up.

"Sit still, Ma," Fred told her.

"I want to."

"You shouldn't go outside, Ma." Fred sat back to show he wasn't moving. "I don't want you outside no more."

"I want to do it, Fred. Mory's right."

Fred was looking at his wife as though he'd just met her.

"I guess I'll have to do it then," he said. "Where'd I put my boots?"

It was not an offer the caretaker made. It was more like a threat. He was looking for Roger to make the next move.

"We'll make it better without you," Roger said.

But Hilda came between them saying, "You're tired, Pa, and I want to get them started. I'm going to do it."

Fred shook his head and picked up the puzzle again.

Hilda did not have to be in the middle of the road because there was no traffic. With the chains Roger made it out easily. From the window Mory watched them go. His mother was waving long after they'd gone.

"They did it," the boy told Fred.

"Big deal," Fred said. "That's all they did. Some company those two were."

"We could get out too, if we had to," Mory said before he closed the curtain and sat down.

Fred looked up from the puzzle. "It's more getting in I'm worried about. With that oil. Where's your mother?"

"Still outside."

"She works too hard," Fred said, looking down at the puzzle.

Mory lay back until he could see the ceiling. For a second he thought about getting up and going to take a bath. He knew he needed to wash himself and at the moment he felt warm water was what he most needed. He could not scrub the burns yet but the water stopped them itching.

Fred consulted one of the dictionaries.

"Where's your mother?" he asked again.

"I don't know," Mory said.

"I swear I don't understand that woman."

Mory lay in the chair thinking of nothing until he was interrupted by sounds like a dog scratching. The noise was definite and he sat up and looked out the window. When he stood up to look over the snowbank, he saw his mother shoveling out the mailbox. As he watched her work in short stiff strokes tossing snow onto the road Mory thought she looked happy. He knew she could not see him watching her and he smiled.

"She's digging out the mailbox," he told Fred.

"What?" Fred was writing down a word carefully and he did not look up.

"I said she's out there shoveling."

"That's sure silly. What does she want to go do that for? There ain't no mail coming today. I was going to do it myself tomorrow if the snow stops. She'll get sick. I know she'll be sick. You watch."

"She don't look sick," Mory said, watching her.

"Your mother hides her sickness. There's lots of times when she's been sick and she didn't look sick because she can hide it. She shouldn't be out there in this weather doing what she's doing."

"Why don't you go tell her?"

Fred opened his dictionary and found another word he needed.

"I knew it," he mumbled. "I just couldn't think of it. I don't know what's the matter with my head today."

Mory continued to watch his mother. Every now and then she would stop and lean on the shovel to check her progress. The snow blew around her boots. When she stopped to brush it off her parka she was like a child shooing a bee. Her blue stocking cap was white with snow and pulled firmly over her head and the string was tight into her chin. Gradually the brown mailbox began to emerge and she worked faster until she could swing it on the pole. He saw her try the flag. Then she began to shovel the turnaround and her stocky body disappeared behind the bank, as though the snow had eaten her. She was shoveling outward toward the narrowed road and she was still working hard. Mory thought her face looked younger and very happy. He was not worried about her when he sat down.

Twenty-One | At three-thirty Hilda came in and made them tea. Fred had not eaten lunch and now he said he was feeling well enough to eat something. He told her to fix cinnamon toast. He had nearly finished his puzzle which made him feel even better.

"I wonder how far they got now," Hilda said, bringing the tea in cups.

"Who?" Fred asked, pulling out the bag and squeezing it.

"Suzanne."

"Quit your worrying, Ma."

"I ain't worrying. I just like to know they're all right."

"Rog is a darn good driver," Mory said. "All you had to see was him get that car out of here. He'll be all right. I bet they're in Watertown before they know it. Then it's all Interstate."

"I know," Hilda said. "That's where we crashed."

"That was different," Fred said, taking a bite of toast. "This tea's hot."

"This time there's more snow," Hilda said. "And I don't like that wind. We didn't have no wind when we hit. You should see the roofs, Fred. Must be two feet up there."

"I seen them," Fred said.

"We used to have nice blizzards like this when I was younger," Hilda said happily. "I used to like them. I remember once I walked right up onto the roof and slid down. It was fun."

"Well, it ain't no fun if you got to shovel them," Fred said. "I thought I'd get away with only having to shovel once this year. Then we get this."

"Did you make your call, Pa?"

"I didn't think of it. I don't know what's the matter with me today. I guess I been too busy. Now I'll have to tell them to send a couple fellows to shovel roofs, too."

Mory said, "The boathouse ain't been cleaned up neither. We got to do that."

Fred said, "Will you come on and stop saying what we got to do, Mory?"

"We probably couldn't get back in there now," Mory said.

"Just leave me worry about what we get in. The oil is the most important. We got to get it in or them pipes'll freeze. Jesus, I wish Weaver'd let me know what he's doing so I could plan."

Mory got up for another cup of tea. He didn't need the tea or its warmth but he thought it was a good idea.

He sat down and leaned back and said, "Here comes that darn wind again."

"Where's that new puzzle?" Fred asked Hilda.

"I ain't seen it."

"I put it right here on the table."

"Maybe somebody moved it."

"Well, somebody had to move it, Hilda, if it was right here on the table where I put it. It didn't move by itself. It didn't go fix itself a sandwich or nothing. I bet one of those stupid kids moved it."

"They don't do puzzles," Hilda said. "They're like me. They ain't got no much education."

"The baby could have moved it," Mory said. "Maybe she ate it."

"Jesus," Fred said again, "I hope they never again bring that kid around here. It ain't her fault. It's her parents. I used to think Joe Ben's kids were bad the way they have to touch everything, but I never seen nothing like that kid of Suzanne's."

"What's the matter with her?" Hilda asked but she got up and turned on the television so they could have something else to discuss.

"She looks like her father and acts like her mother," Fred said. He was pleased with himself. "That's what's the matter. That's enough."

"She's just a baby."

Mory couldn't help laughing but he was laughing alone.

"I ain't making jokes," Fred said. "It's serious and

somebody ought to tell them. They ain't my kids and I don't
want nothing to do with them or I'd tell them."

Fred made a gesture with the pencil to indicate his
disgust.

"They were lucky to have the baby," Mory said.

"That's right, Pa. It was like a gift."

"Yeah, who from? Anyhow, that baby ain't lucky to
have them. You'd think for someone who had such a hard
time getting herself knocked up permanent and had all
them busted miscarriages, she'd take a little care of the one
she got."

"Fred," Hilda said firmly, her only way of scolding him.

"No, I mean it, Hilda. She don't even know how to
burp the kid right. Did you see the way she lets it pee itself?
Probably would let it crap itself too, if we wasn't here."

Mory wanted to laugh again but the lines on Fred's
face were tightening. In the chair, the boy was prepared for
anything.

"It ain't funny," Fred said, looking over at Mory. "It's
serious. That kid don't have a chance to act decent. It ain't
her fault."

"What'd she do that's so bad?" Mory asked.

"Listen, I'm telling you and you won't listen."

Mory saw his mother turn her attention to the television.

"Maybe you didn't know, Mory, because you was
young then. And you was always a clean kid. We always was
able to teach you right. But them brothers and sisters of
yours was filthy when they come here. Wasn't they Hilda?"

Mory's mother nodded quickly. Suddenly the boy was
sorry for her. It was like being in the snow. Fred went on
and they had to leave or listen.

"And what they married ain't much better. You can't
even look at Joe Ben's wife with them teeth of hers. Looks
like she was chewing tobacco. I told him to have her get

them fixed. You think he'd do it? All he wants her for is to fuck. Even John said he had her first."

"It was going to cost them too much money," Mory said.

"Yeah, well, I don't like her," Fred said. "And I don't like that slippery little Sara either. But at least they ain't mean like Suzanne. I never knew a kid so mean to her mother. Remember that dress you made her, Ma?"

Hilda wasn't listening to him so he leaned up and poked her in the ribs. She flinched and turned around sharply.

"Remember how you spent all that time making that pretty dress for Suzanne and when it was done she wouldn't wear it to the prom because the skirt wasn't short enough to suit her fancy ass? Right up to her butt, she wanted it. Like some whore selling it."

"All the girls was wearing short dresses that year, Fred. It was the fashion then. Even the ladies wore them."

"Well it ain't right for none of them. Not for nice clean people. Wearing those provocative clothes so you can see their bushes. What if all the men went around with their sausages hanging out? Would you do that, Mory?"

"No," the boy said. He was holding his guts and wanting to laugh hard.

"Well, that's what I'm saying. What if I got myself one of them tight swim suits that the swimmers wear and walked around town wagging my ass? What then? I'll tell you what. They'd put me in jail. I bet they would. People ain't got no morals anymore. I don't know what to make of it. I give up."

Fred sat back. He had already exhausted himself but he wasn't through. He would let them know when he was through.

"You know what really burns me up?"

"What?" Mory said so they could hear him out quickly.

"It's what's the matter with this whole goddamn country today. You can see it on the television. The kids ain't got no respect for nothing and nobody. They don't show no decency. You've seen them outdoor music festivals they have. Pig parties, I call them. What do they do? First they get themselves high on all that dope so they don't know nothing anyway. Then they strip off all their clothes so they're bare-assed naked. Can you imagine that? Then they lie around fucking in the grass and flaunting authority and then they go take a bath in a lake filled with so much puss and crap that even a cow wouldn't use it. All that lousy come in there and they're swimming in it. Yeah, and then they try to tell us how to run things. Like they knew stuff that we ain't never learned. They ought to take the whole bunch of them kids and ship their naked asses over to the snow fields in Red China or wherever it is. Just like the niggers. These kids today are nothing but a bunch of niggers."

"They ain't hurting nobody but themselves," Hilda said. "That dope is awful."

"Yeah, and you got that dope right in school, don't you, Mory?"

The boy was looking out the window. The sky was darkening quickly. The snow was gray.

"Mory don't take dope," Hilda said. "He ain't even in school this year."

"You think he'd say if he did? No. They got a code not to tell. But it's there. I know it is. The teachers is selling it."

"It's there," Mory said.

"See, Ma? At least he tells us."

"But I never used it," Mory said.

"Well, you got decency, Mory. You ain't like the rest. You keep in shape and you got respect. Now, Suzanne, she never had respect for nobody. God knows what she's done. And that Roger ain't much better. Acts like's he so smart.

Look at how they got married. Eloping. And knocked up, too. After we'd ordered all them flowers special, and had them invitations and match books printed up. Of course, I blame his parents for that. They're just trash. Yeah, and they think they're too good for us. Right, Ma?"

"I don't like neither of them," Hilda said.

Suzanne's wedding remained a very sore point for Hilda. She had planned it as nicely as she could, like the party. She and Fred had spent their money and time for it. They had asked all their friends and even some of the wealthy camp owners who knew Fred. Everybody had sent presents. Then there had been complications with Roger's family about where they would stay and Fred had gotten into the thick of it. Finally all Roger's family refused to come. Then Roger and Suzanne eloped to Massena and Fred and Hilda had to return all the presents. Two weeks later Suzanne miscarried the first time.

"We had it all planned so nice," Hilda said, remembering. "I cried for three days."

"I know you did, Ma, and you should have. I never knew such shits in my life as them Bettors."

"They didn't even tell us," Hilda said. She looked ready to cry again over the memory.

"That's what I'm saying," Fred said.

Then the caretaker really noticed his wife's mood and he set up and said, "Shit, Ma, my back's hurting me again. I don't know what it is. I didn't eat no lunch."

Suddenly the room was like a spinnaker losing wind. Hilda turned on a light.

"Maybe you should go lay down, Fred. I could call you when dinner's ready."

"I'm going to take a bath," Mory said, standing up.

"I don't want to miss my news, Ma. Not like last night."

Fred was standing up, too, so Hilda stood up.

"I think I might lay down for a little while."

"I'll get you up for the news."

"Thanks, Mommy."

Mory walked past them both and he could feel his head again where Fred had hit him.

Twenty-Two | The lights went out halfway through Walter Cronkite's report. Cronkite was reporting the American retreat from Vietnam. Most of it was old, sad news.

They were eating leftovers, the fat end of a ham, creamed corn, some salad, milk and pie. The coffee was waiting on the stove, already hot. The meal had been pleasant without conversation. Suddenly they were in the dark, watching the newscaster's head shrink and die.

"Well, shit," said Fred with a full mouth of cherry pie. "I knew it. Where's my flashlight, Ma?"

"I seen it yesterday," Hilda said. "Where was it?"

Nobody moved. The sitting room was strangely peaceful, as though all things had drained from their lives with the electric current, and finally they could rest. Then they began to hear the storm again outside naturally, and as they sat and waited for something else to happen, their initial sense of release gave way to gloom.

"I hope it don't last too long," Hilda said.

Mory felt himself shiver.

"I wonder how long before they fix it," Fred said. His teeth snapped when he swallowed. In the darkness his voice sounded louder. "Probably be a while before they can find the break and get to it. I wouldn't want to be no lineman tonight."

"Should we call?" Hilda asked.

"Probably took the phone lines with it. One of them big icy branches cracks and it can take everything out."

Fred spoke clearly, as though he were discussing the war with Cronkite.

"What'll we do?" Hilda asked.

"We can't do nothing, Ma. We just got to wait."

"You all right, Mory? You ain't said a peep."

"Sure," Mory said. "I finished eating."

"Did you finish, Fred?"

"All but my pie. I can't eat no more. That was real good, Ma."

"It wasn't nothing," Hilda said.

"Where'd we buy that ham?" Fred asked. "I'm going to get us a couple more. We can keep them for emergencies."

"The Supply," Hilda said. "Remember, you didn't like those ones we got to the A & P?"

"Yeah, they was all fat and gristle," Fred said into the darkness. "But these ones are good."

The caretaker might have been any place in the room. The room might have been anywhere and any size. It didn't matter. For a moment the darkness and the storm had brought them together.

Then Mory moved and said, "I'll get my light."

"Be careful," said Hilda. "Don't bump your head."

"Watch the tables," said Fred.

They heard Mory leave his lounger and start walking toward them. He had his hands stretched out in front. Then they heard the red mouse squeak as Mory stepped on it. They knew he was near the television.

"Watch yourself, Mickey," Fred said and they laughed.

Mory reached the doorway close to Hilda and stopped. He saw a glow from the stove burner and he smelled the coffee. He stepped out in the kitchen and turned into the hallway. His balance was not good. He was feeling air with his hands as he crept along the walls to his room. He knew exactly where the flashlight was and he came back to the kitchen quickly. Fred joined him and they went down to the cellar to find the Coleman lanterns. Mory held the light as Fred filled them. Then there was enough light.

When Hilda could see, she poured coffee at the kitchen table. Fred went into their bedroom and brought back the transistor radio. They sat around the table to drink coffee and listen to weather reports.

The situation was worsening throughout the Adirondacks. The radio advised people not to drive except in extreme emergencies. There had been numerous accidents already. One involved a potato farmer and his tractor. Another a Saranac Lake policeman on patrol. That afternoon a baby had been delivered by its father at an abandoned roadside fruit stand. Both the mother and child were doing well. Niagara Mohawk was working through the night to restore power to those areas stricken by the blizzard. Heat should be conserved at all costs. People were advised to stay in their homes and not to go outside for anything but essentials. The storm would slacken by morning. Then there was music.

"Let's see if this phone does work," Fred said. "What's Bill Schoolman's number?"

"I've forgot," said Hilda happily.

When Fred went to the phone, Hilda got out her largest kettle and put enough water on the stove to do the dishes. Mory collected the plates from the sitting room.

Fred set the phone book on the table. He was whistling while he found Schoolman's number with his forefinger. He dialed and put the phone to his ear.

"I hope he ain't been drinking," Fred said. "Hello, Bill?"

Hilda produced the two large plastic tubs from somewhere and placed them in the sink. She put all the dishes and silverware in one and squirted out some detergent.

"Pretty good, old boy. Say, we got a bit of a problem up here."

Mory sat down.

"Yeah, we just lost them, too. Burns me up. Yeah, I was watching the news. But that's not what I was calling about."

"Schoolman must be out of his electricity, too," Hilda told Mory. She was standing by the stove and listening to Fred talk, and waiting for the water to boil.

"Say, you know that truck I got? Well, I can't do nothing with it no more. It's plumb shot and I got to keep that road of mine plowed to the boss's cabin. Why? So's I can get in oil to the furnace. You think you can help me? Sure. It was low last week, too. I ain't checked it since. Well, I told them to come but they must have forgot."

Hilda tested the water with her finger. It could not possibly have boiled yet.

"The grader? What'll it cost me? I know I don't pay no bills but I got to answer for them. My boss ain't no Onassis neither. At least I ain't never seen him act like one. Hilda wasn't married to no president before I found her either."

Fred laughed into the phone.

"What time in the morning? I know I ain't going nowhere. O.K., old boy, and I'll buy you a drink when you're through."

Fred hung up the phone.

"He'll be around with the grader in the morning. He thinks we'll need a back hoe to get in close to the house. He don't know what he can do if we get any more snow."

"You do what you have to do, Fred," Hilda said. At last she could pour the water into the tubs. Mory found a towel to dry.

When the dishes were done, Fred took his radio into

the bedroom and lay down. He wanted to listen to CBS in New York. At night the New York station was clearer than other broadcasts and he had all his news all the time. When he couldn't fish or watch television in the evenings, he preferred lying in bed listening to the radio. Hilda had her own small transistor and she would listen to WWVA with an earplug when Fred was tuned in elsewhere.

Mory grabbed the other lantern and went into the living room. Hilda brought her sewing kit and they sat on the couch together with the light glowing on the table between them. Across the room the bay window was like a black block of natural ice.

Hilda seemed less nervous but she fumbled through the wicker basket of buttons, bobbins, spools, and needles. It was a mess. She had one of Fred's woolen shirts on her lap.

"I like losing the lights like this," Mory said. "It kind of puts you in your place."

Hilda found the button she wanted. She squinted when she threaded the needle.

"You know, Mory, when I was your age, we never did have no electricity. All's we had for heat was a wood stove and, if that weren't enough, we had to get into bed. They were days when my mother didn't let us out of bed all day."

"What about school?" the boy asked.

His mother had told him about herself many times but he felt she wanted to bring it up again. He was very close to her.

"We was like you," his mother said. "Only we wasn't injured. We just didn't go to school much."

"Why not?"

"Because," Hilda said, jabbing the needle through the button, "for one thing there wasn't no yellow buses yet and we had to walk to get there. We wasn't as far from school as this camp is but it was a long walk. For the next thing, we didn't like learning much."

"Didn't they come after you?"

"Who did?"

"The truant officers."

"They didn't want to come see us any more than we wanted to go see them. You know how your grandpa can be when he wants to."

Mory remembered last night and his grandfather's face on the floor. Even without moving, the old man could look tough and resentful.

"Then you met my father," Mory said slowly.

"He was working," Hilda said, remembering. "He was a smart man. He had two steady jobs and he'd do guiding in his spare time. He could have gone to college. He was sure a powerful good looking man, Mory. Handsome, like you are. One fall when I first went with him, he cut all our winter wood. Your grandpa said he was a good man to do that. You know how your grandpa is about people. He don't say much and he don't like nobody or nothing he don't have to."

"What was the matter with him?" the boy asked.

He watched his mother's hands and thought how they would have been good skillful hands, like a machinist's, without the arthritis.

"What was the matter with who, Mory?"

"With my father. How come he left?"

"I told you before. He didn't never say. He just left. He had to go to that war in Korea and when he come back he wasn't the same man. First he was going to stay in the Army for his life but then he got his honorable discharge. But he didn't want to work no more. Nothing seemed to please him after that except his hunting and fishing, and driving the car he bought. He was sure some driver. He just drove away. I can see him now."

"I wish I knew where he was now," Mory said.

"What could you do if you knew, Mory?"

"Go find him."

"What would you say? Your father was quite a talker. He could have given speeches."

"I'd tell him who I was. What do you think he'd do then?"

"I don't know, Mory. He'd know you were his boy. You've growed to look like him. Sometimes when I watch you I see your father in you. You was the only one who got his yellow hair. He had such nice long yellow hair, and his beard was bright red when he let it grow. He was a sight."

"Could we find him if we had to?"

"Maybe we could. Only he ain't ours no more, Mory. Lord knows where he is."

Hilda broke the thread with her fingers.

"He is, too, ours," Mory said. "He's mine."

"He don't seem to think so. You don't want to be thinking about your real dad, Mory. You can't do nothing about him so you want to leave him be. Like he was dead."

"But he ain't dead and sometimes I can't quit thinking about him. He never even come around once. I ain't never even seen him."

"Look in the mirror. You'll see him."

"I hope I'm not like him," the boy said. "I hope I'm never like him. And I don't want to look like him. Does he have scars like mine?"

"He never did."

"Then I'm not like him. I'm not like anybody else. Nobody else has got these scars like I do."

"Quit talking about your scars. It ain't nice."

"But they're mine," Mory said and he was about to beat his fists into his thighs.

"What's the matter, Mory?" Hilda asked. "You're acting funny."

"I don't know," the boy said. "Sometimes I don't even know who I am. Or why I'm here. Or where I'm going. I don't know anything."

"That's silly," Hilda said holding up the shirt to admire her work. "You shouldn't try to think about things like that."

Wind struck the bay window. The glass rattled in the frame. The snow was turning icy now and the boy and his mother could hear it fall, like bits of dry corn on paper.

"You're just Mory Keller," Hilda said. "And you're the youngest, and you're going to grow up the best."

The lantern flickered and the glow retreated briefly to the globe, leaving them darkness. Then the generator cleared itself and they could see each other, mother and son, tired and worn out together.

"I wish I knew," Mory said.

"Knew what?"

"If that was who I was."

Hilda looked at him.

"I don't know," she said, "but it don't matter."

Twenty-Three | Mory put on his pajama bottoms and went into the bathroom to wash. When he was washed he stood before the mirror watching himself darkly by the lantern light. He was not exactly sure what he was looking for but he looked long and hard. If, as his mother had said, there was another person there whom he had never known, he did not recognize him. He saw only himself.

There were things bothering his mind when Mory returned to his room so he picked up the barbell and began doing curls. He did not bother to count the repetitions. He performed the exercises methodically and smoothly and stared at the cold window as though it held his future. Only when he felt the weights pulling him and saw the veins risen hard in his arms and felt himself about to perspire did Mory stop and put on his pajama top. When he looked around the room he was unable to see into the dark corners.

Then the boy turned off the lantern and jumped into bed. As the glow sputtered and died, he could hear nothing but himself breathing heavily. Then the mantle lost itself and he saw he had left the door partly open. He could see the faint glow from Hilda's lantern and he could not sleep yet.

Jimmy came silently into the room on the prowl for warmth. The boy barely heard the cat jump onto his bed but he felt him lay down lightly at his hip. He reached out to touch the cat's head, feeling the soft ears, and the fine long hairs folding under his fingers. Someone had once told Mory how a cat would eat him if he died but tonight that hardly seemed likely.

Jimmy was a close friend and he no longer traveled much. There had been difficult times for Mory when the cat disappeared for weeks and the boy would fear he had been shot, or crushed on the road, or caught in a trap. After searching under all the cabins he would wait anxiously for the cat's return. Hilda would tell him not to worry and Fred would insist that the cat knew what he was doing. He needed his fun, Fred would say shyly.

Eventually the boy learned to understand the cat and how he behaved and what he needed. Then they collaborated on grand schemes. The schemes were a boy's dreams and the cat was a good partner. He would never reveal the boy's plans and he would carry most of them out when he was gone. Then as they aged Mory came to feel that Jimmy was losing interest. They collaborated less and the boy realized the cat no longer traveled so much to hunt or find a mate, but rather because he needed to travel while he could. It was a bad sign. The cat still needed to go away

very much but less now, and he had this place to return to
which was easy.

Sometimes Mory was hurt because he could not go
with Jim. He had never really been anywhere. His longest
trips outside the Adirondacks were to Malone and Ithaca.
They were just visits or for shopping and they had been
short trips. Once his class had gone to Montreal for a hockey
match but he had stayed home because Hilda was sick. Last
year his class had planned to go to New York on a bus but
the trip was cancelled by snow. He didn't know where the
class went this year and now he wondered where they might
go next. Then he realized he would be in another class next
year. This thought hurt him.

There in the night Mory realized how the accident had
spoiled everything. It had scooped him up, ruined his
relation to everything he knew, and dropped him down
where he didn't belong.

He sat up in bed. He was very alone.

He had heard the doctors say the damage wouldn't be
permanent but they couldn't know his mind. Right now his
head didn't seem to understand that his body would heal.
He had just been sprung from one black pot to another.
Even if he were on his own now, he couldn't move from
where he was. That thought hurt most of all. That was
terrifying. Particularly in the lonely night.

Jimmy had been everywhere he wanted to go. Now he
was content to stand still, to sit by the stove, to lay on
Mory's bed, to let his territory shrink to the house. But Mory
would want to begin moving, away from the house, into
new places, maybe to never return if he found someplace
better. And he knew he could not. He was stranded there
with himself and he had been nowhere yet. He could do
nothing.

Mory felt too warm and got up to open the window.

After the exercise, the window was light as a feather. Outside the wind was gone and he could barely hear the snow. He came back to bed and lay down without bothering the cat.

Then he was thinking of Samuel Weaver and how he too had traveled everywhere he wanted. Weaver did not act as old as Jimmy but he was approaching the point where he was satisfied to spend his holidays at the camp rather than to travel anymore. When Weaver returned from trips, Mory would wait and select the right moment to ask questions. Or, if Weaver was busy and his sons had gone along, he would ask them.

Weaver could tell the boy of Florida and Montana and California and of great places outside America, and of why those lands were different, and the people, and what they did. Usually when they talked Weaver would be sitting on his open porch with the good strong view of Mt. Marcy across the lake, and the man would lay out his memories in a fine long string. The boy would hear a distant surf or a shale slide starting or the slap a marlin makes when he hits the outrigger bait, and Mory would absorb those sounds like good advice. Sometimes a powerboat would venture too close to camp while Weaver was speaking and then the big man would stand and shake his fist at the driver and yell and the memories would end there sadly. Then Weaver would shake his head and sit down and point his finger after the intruders and say they were why the Upper Saranac could never be perfect. Mory wouldn't understand and he would listen to the man fall off into cursing the general public and conclude with a condemnation of the whole world he had seen.

But Mory loved this other world without seeing it. He knew the general public only as he saw and understood it from the grass, or on long walks with Hilda when she needed to lose weight. He knew certain people from school and town and he saw others on the road but he had not met this damned public of Weaver's or seen their places. He was young and eager and just awakening as he recovered, and everything which he did not have seemed to be much better than what he had. Sometimes he wanted to find out all things for himself very much. Often he felt if he could just get going his life would change for the better. He did not think he could be wrong.

When the room cooled down, Jimmy left for the stove.

Mory had confused himself by thinking. He turned over on his stomach to fall asleep. His last thoughts were of camp wood smoke and of how he would be well enough to fish when the ice went out.

Twenty-Four | Fred was up fairly early.

"Payday," he shouted at Mory's door. He was on his way to the kitchen. He didn't explain.

Mory rolled over in bed. When he opened his eyes, he thought it wasn't snowing. Then he saw he was wrong. The snow fell in a loose shower. The fragile flakes were barely visible, caught here and there by breeze, like bits of leaf. The sky had lifted somewhat and Mory could see dark trees on the hill.

Mory's feet hit the floor heavily. The room was cold. He had slept too well and now he felt drugged. Somehow this day was different. When he dressed in the same clothes and went into the kitchen, he walked like a patient the day before surgery. Sleep was still in his eyes.

"Today we should get going," Fred was saying. Hilda poured his coffee. The caretaker was wearing his onepiece longjohns. The top buttons were open. As usual he was without his shirt.

"Any lights yet?" Mory asked sitting down.

"You want your orange juice or your coffee first?" Hilda asked.

"We don't need no lights now," Fred said. "What's the matter with your eyes, kid? Can't you see yet?"

For some reason Fred was in high gear.

"Orange juice," Mory said sourly.

"Bill comes and I'll have him open us a road good as if I'd done it myself."

"Where we going?"

"Can't tell. That grader is what we need. I wonder why I didn't think of that before."

"You want two eggs or one, Pa?"

"Two's fine, Ma. Got to work today. No sense in having Bill bother with the boathouse. Just in here and on out to the boss's shack. I wonder though, as long as he's here, we ain't cleaned up after ourselves over there yet, have we?"

"No," said Mory. He drank his orange juice in one gulp.

"I'll go over, Fred. I can borrow Mr. Weaver's snowshoes. He won't know I done it."

"I don't want you going over there, Ma. You done too much already, and I don't want you tiring yourself out in that deep snow, like it is."

"Mory can go with me. Would you like that, Mory?"

Mory was thinking of something else so he didn't answer.

Fred smiled and sipped his coffee. "Hilda, I don't want you over there."

"But it might get to stinking, Fred," the woman said. She was frying bacon and it sizzled. "Those smells is hard to get out if you let them stay forever. Particularly in them rugs."

"What smells? Ma, it's like an ice box in there. Ain't no smells if everything's frozen."

"I know," she said, "but I got to do something."

Bill Schoolman arrived with his grader while they were eating. They heard him drop the blade and begin to make the first cut in from the road to the house. Then the house shook and they saw the enormous tires through the window. Bill got off the machine and came in the house for coffee.

"Morning, old boy," Fred said.

"Morning, Fred. Hilda. Mory."

"Morning."

"Morning."

"Yes, it is," Bill said, grinning. "Another one."

Hilda said, "Sit down, Bill. Have coffee."

"Thanks," said Bill.

"Cold out?" Fred asked.

"Colder than yesterday. Not as much wind though."

"Not hardly."

"Storm's getting done with."

"Could be at that."

"Been a bad one."

"Could have been worse."

"Worst one this year."

"Could be. Four folks died near Malone. I heard it on the radio this morning."

"I ain't heard my radio this morning."

"Said a man and his wife and the two kids. Said the car give out and they had to stay there. Kept the heater on. Asphyxiated them. They plumb froze up. Like four trout in the deep freeze, it sounded like, when they dug them out."

"Oh, no," said Hilda as if the victims had been her own.

"Yep, the way they told it," Bill said nodding.

Bill Schoolman's hand shook when he reached for the coffee. For sixteen hours each day he was a determined alcoholic. He slept for six more and the other two he was able to work. If he had anything to say about it, his work was mainly supervisory. Normally, when he woke, he would jump into his pickup and check on the few camps he looked after, or the few men he had placed on the few jobs he was offered. Then the bars were open.

The construction company which Bill had taken over from his former boss had been a going, if seasonal, concern. Now, under Bill's leadership, it was headed downhill rapidly. There were no new materials in the mill and most of the equipment had turned the corner into old age. Somehow he managed to contract and complete enough work to make his payments and to keep the banks from bothering him. He was a sight. During the winter he rarely changed his clothes. Frequently he missed his shave. He had worn gray Malone trousers and a green checked wool hunting cap and jacket for as long as most people cared to remember. He was a bachelor by necessity so few people knew what he wore underneath. Some said nothing.

Now Bill's hand kept shaking as he raised the coffee cup to his mouth and lowered it. His lips were painfully cracked and the gray sprouts of his unshaved beard reflected light. If the house had not been cold, he may have smelled. Yet his eyes were clear and active beneath the caked brim of the hunting cap he never removed. Bill Schoolman was the sort of northcountry person who might do anything for a friend, or who might do nothing, and he was thoroughly dependable for the first two hours of every day.

"What's it you have in mind, Fred?" he asked.

Fred pushed aside his plate.

"I got to get my road open to the boss's cabin. I could have done it myself if it wasn't for that damn truck."

"Giving you trouble?"

"What ain't these days, Bill?"

"You just want me to cut a road?"

"We got to be able to get out, too. If you can plow the

area here by the garage and woodshed so's I can get my car out, and then make us a road to the highway."

"We'll see," Bill said slowly, as though he might not. "How you going to get the oil from the road to the house? Where's the fillspout?"

"It's there," Fred said. "I can show it to you. I guess I got to dig it out. It's maybe thirty feet from where I quit plowing with the truck. You'll see. Under a window."

"Near them trees?"

"Yeah, under a window."

"A man's going to have to get in there with a hose," Bill said, thinking it over. "And I can't make it under them trees with Old Yellow."

"Be close," Fred said, nodding.

They were like field grade officers planning an assault they wouldn't have to join.

"I could get the back hoe in there if I had it."

"I thought you was bringing it."

"Wasn't sure if you needed it. It'll cost you."

"Let it cost," Fred said. "What doesn't?"

"Your phone still working? I'll call Barney. See if he's at the mill yet."

"Try it."

Bill dialed the mill. Hilda stood up to collect the breakfast dishes. She listened to Bill ask Barney to bring the back hoe. She was dressed only in her robe, nightgown, and slippers. She wore no makeup. Outside Bill's grader ran on relentlessly.

Bill hung up and said, "I heard you folks had quite a party the other night." He sat down to drink more coffee.

"It was a real nice party," Hilda said.

"Until the end," Fred said quietly. "Then it sort of collapsed. It was embarrassing but we couldn't do nothing about it."

Bill nodded. "Too bad about your dad, Hilda. I heard it on the radio. How's he doing?"

"We ain't heard," Fred said. "We ain't had no time for news. And with this storm we couldn't go find out for ourselves."

"You should have come to the party, Bill," Hilda said.

"I would have come," Bill said. He was going to add something but he tapped Mory's shoulder in what was intended to be a friendly gesture. "Did you go, youngster?"

"I went," Mory said, "for a while."

"He come in at the end," Fred said. "He was there for the fireworks part."

"That's too bad," Bill said slowly. He was nodding at Mory. "Well, I guess I got to get out there."

"Let me know if I can help," Fred said.

"When Barney comes with the other machine, you can show him where the pipe is so he don't bust it off. I should have her open back into there by then."

"O.K., old boy. Stop by for a snort on your way out."

"I'll do that," Bill said.

Twenty-Five | When Fred and Mory went into the living room to begin the day in earnest, Hilda left the breakfast dishes unwashed in the plastic tubs and went to dress.

The snow was falling more and more sparsely. It seemed as though the sky were exhausted. Now it had drained itself to the point where a plane could fly visually with some degree of safety.

The grader groaned as it ground into the blizzard's residue. It lurched like a wounded horse dragging itself and the plowed snow trailed high off the sloped edge of the blade. In places near the buildings the banks rose almost to the bottom of the cab.

Fred worked a lamp switch but the current was still out.

Mory thumbed the Montgomery Ward catalogue. He lingered only at the sports equipment section and the ladies underwear.

"Let's see what it says in the paper," Fred said, picking up last Friday's edition. He put it down quickly.

"What'd it say?" Mory asked from behind the wishing book.

"Nothing."

"It says here you can buy a plastic swimming pool real cheap."

"We already got a lake."

"It ain't ours."

"Thank God. Next thing you know the boss would want me to cut ice and sell it."

"I think next year for Christmas I'm going to buy you a pair of these striped bell bottoms," Mory said.

For a second Fred may have thought the boy was serious because he didn't react immediately. Then he said, "Save your money. I don't want to look like a fairy."

"You ever try sandals?" the boy asked. He was pressing the old man safely.

"Jesus Christ," said the caretaker. "If I wanted to look like a woman, I'd buy me a dress."

"And let your hair grow, huh?"

"Yeah, and get me one of them Maidenform Bras."

"Why, Fred Macken, you dirty old man," Hilda said.

She was standing silently in the doorway. She was smiling and dressed in her ski clothes. With her stocking cap and no makeup, she could have been a fat, happy, middle-aged man.

"Mory started it," the caretaker said defensively but his amusement hid his embarrassment.

"What's he doing to you, Pa?"

"Trying to make me a fairy or something."

"Don't you think Fred would look great in bell bottoms and sandals?" Mory asked his mother. The boy laughed as he visualized the outfit. "It would be better than a bikini."

He had to laugh at that, too.

"Oh, Mory," Hilda said. She was laughing.

"What's so funny?" Fred asked. "Quit your darn picking on me."

"You in a bikini," Hilda said and she couldn't stop laughing.

"Well?"

"I don't think you better get no bikini, Pa."

"Why in hell not?" Fred pretended to be insulted.

Mory was still chuckling.

"I'd look as good as some of these women wearing them."

"You ain't no woman, Fred," Hilda said.

"All right, Ma," Fred said. "Now where you think you're going dressed like that?"

The joking was ended.

"Outside," Hilda said.

"I told you I don't want you going out there. What's to do outside anyway?"

"Shovel the mailbox," Hilda said. Suddenly she was reduced to a little girl, answering questions and guilty of something.

"Look, Ma, quit worrying about the mailbox. There ain't going to be no mail today neither."

"All right," she said. "I'll just see what Bill's doing. I like to watch him work that equipment piece."

After he let her go, Fred told Mory, "With all these

years that woman still don't listen to me." He didn't sound annoyed.

"She don't even pay no attention to herself," he said.

Soon Mory saw his mother at the mailbox with the coal shovel. Fred didn't notice her until Barney Cullen arrived with the back hoe. He just shook his head. Then he had to go outside to find the fillspout.

"Goddamn snow," the caretaker said, clomping out in his overshoes.

Mory was into appliances.

Twenty-Six | Bill Schoolman drank three quick shots of Fred's best bourbon while Barney Cullen drank his one slowly with a water chaser. Both men cleared their throats and stopped shivering. They had no more frost in their ears when they left the camp on their heavy machinery.

The driveway was clear from the highway to Weaver's cabin. There was a footpath to the fillspout. Between the pumphouse and the woodshed the banks touched the gutters. From there back to Weaver's cabin, the access road resembled a huge bobsled straightway, with a sharp curve at the edge of the garden and a gentler one at the corner of the guest cabin. The track was mostly old snow but it was at least three feet deep.

"Well, that's that," said Fred. He was seriously considering another shot. "I like old Bill. He ain't so bad as everybody says. He always done good by me. Maybe he drinks too much but so what? He's sure a damn sight better worker than most of them people who talk him down."

"He done a real nice job, Fred," said Hilda. She had declined to drink with the men.

Fred tipped the bottle and watched his hand pour another.

"Yeah, people is always finding fault with old Bill but they ain't much better."

"Niagara Mohawk certainly ain't much better," said Mory. "I don't know which is worse when it comes to repairs, them or the phone company."

Mory had gone outside to watch the men finish and he still wore his thick white sweater.

"Be close," Fred said. "Maybe I should give them a call. You don't suppose they forgot about us?"

"I'm going to call the hospital and find out," Hilda said vaguely. She wasn't doing anything else.

"Don't worry, Ma. They'd have called us if anything happened. Your dad's O.K. He's tougher than a boot anyway."

"But I feel stupid not calling before. People is going to think we don't care."

"Let them think," Fred said. "It's good for them. Anyhow now I can run you in to see him if you want. Would you like that, Ma?"

"There's some things we could get in town, too," Hilda said.

"What do we need, Ma? Should we go? I'd sure like getting out of here before it drives me nuts."

"I already feel like the fact we're able to go after the storm has come makes us like the convicts when they're released somewhere," Hilda said. "It's like maybe we shouldn't spoil our liberty when we get it."

"What're you talking about, Mommy?" Fred said, as he considered his wife's mouthful.

"You know what I mean, Pa. Maybe I didn't say it just right."

"You been drinking, Ma?"

Hilda fidgeted and laughed.

"Should we do it, Mory?" Fred asked.

"Do what," Mory said. He thought the fact they were able to leave the house hadn't altered his life one bit. He could not share in their enthusiasm.

"Go see how your grandfather's doing this afternoon?"

"Shouldn't we call to see if he wants to see us?"

"No, we'll just surprise the old-timer."

"Let's," Hilda said eagerly.

"Maybe the roads ain't clear yet," said Mory.

"Bill didn't have no trouble. He'd of said something."

"The television don't work noway," Hilda said.

"That's right. We can have our dinner in town and by the time we get back, I bet everything's working again."

"Where we going to eat, Pa?" Hilda asked. She was on the road already.

"Maybe the hotel. No, I don't like the hotel. The food's lousy. The service is O.K. because them kids there do try. They just don't know nothing yet. But the food stinks. Remember them chops I had there?"

"Which ones?"

Hilda honestly could not have remembered.

"Them little ones. I really wanted chops that night. Remember? When they come they was so small I couldn't see them. Just two bones. They was pork. I never been so disappointed. I think you had the fish and it wasn't no good neither."

"Now I remember," Hilda said but her memory was highly questionable. "Do you want me to fix you a sandwich? There's egg salad and soda crackers."

"Maybe later, Ma. I don't feel like eating yet. I got a little cold digging out there."

"Where would you like to eat tonight, Mory?"

Mory was far away, thinking of other places. He had to come back quickly.

"Florida," the boy said.

They all laughed at his answer.

"I mean if you can't eat to Florida," Hilda said, laughing.

"Dew Drop's," Mory said.

"You like that place?" Fred asked.

"I like their spaghetti with sausage and peppers," Mory said. "And I like going down to get there and having to come up to get out."

"You're talking like your mother. You just like it because it's near the theatre."

"No, I enjoy it because it's like a place you read about. Every time I go there it's like a place I never been."

"You been there a lot," Fred said. "It's kind of greasy."

The restaurant in question was on the main street at the center of town. You ate below street level, right over the Saranac River. There were ducks in the river and it was a pleasant place to eat.

"We could go to the show," Hilda said. She was hoping to expand their plans enough to excite Mory.

"What's playing?" Fred asked. He preferred going in summer to the Sara-Placid Drive-In because it was cheaper.

"Probably something X-rated," Mory said.

"Yeah, I don't know why they do that."

"Maybe it's a western," Hilda said. "We could call and find out."

"You sure want to call someone, don't you, Ma?"

"If it ain't X-rated, it's a Disney," Mory said.

"Want me to call?"

"I don't know," the caretaker said. "I didn't care much for that last one we saw. It was supposed to be for the general family but you still saw that girl's titty. She was cute enough but I don't know why they think they have to do that."

"What was the name of it?" Hilda asked.

"You remember. It had Robert Mitchum starring. He's always good but in this one he didn't do much. He was the school teacher in Ireland that married the girl younger than him that took up with the Army man. Remember, they cut her hair off in the end? Them other women was like savages."

"*Ryan's Daughter*," Mory said.

"That's it," Hilda said. "*Ryan's Daughter*. Ryan was the bartender who done the bad thing. You wanted to see that one, didn't you Mory?"

"You liked the music," Mory said.

"But we went special for you."

"It was a good picture. Mr. Weaver told me to go. He said it was better than *Dr. Zhivago*. He seen *Dr. Zhivago* four times."

"I liked *Dr. Zhivago*, too," Hilda said. "Nobody can't play that song better than Chet Atkins."

"*Ryan's Daughter* was almost as good," Mory said.

"It was too long," Fred said. He had ruled out the movies but he noticed Hilda's disappointment and said, "Maybe we should just go to Florida. Would you like that, Ma?"

"Oh, Fred," Hilda said. "Quit your teasing."

"Who's teasing? We ain't had no vacation in three years."

"We ain't been to Florida in five."

"Suzanne ruined that trip. It would have been so nice without her. Remember how much you liked them bands in that parade, Ma?"

"You remember them big double shots at that nice bar?"

"Yeah, and cheap, too."

"I wish we could go, Pa. We'd all feel better."

"Just watching them bikinis makes me feel good."

"Remember them big sharks they was catching at night out off the pier on the boardwalk? That didn't make me feel too good. But you sure liked them, Mory, remember?"

"Who's going to watch this place?" Mory asked.

Fred drained his glass. "He's right, Ma. We can't go nowhere. We're stuck here. Maybe next year we can get away."

"Would you care for a sandwich now, Fred?"

"Maybe I could try a little one, Ma. Some of that bologna, if we got any left. I don't want no egg salad."

Hilda hummed the theme from *Dr. Zhivago* as she made their lunch. They didn't notice when the snow stopped.

When they finished, Fred told Hilda to make up a shopping list for later. He said he was going to lay down for a while. Then they would go to town.

"I ain't going with you," Mory told his mother later.

"Why not? Don't you want to go? We'll just see your grandpa and do a little shopping and then have our dinner. We'll have a nice dinner somewhere."

"I don't want to go," Mory said.

"You feel all right? You didn't catch no cold out there?"

"I don't have nothing to do in town," Mory said. The thought of making the trip irked him. Going anywhere was just an illusion. His grandfather wasn't dead yet and he didn't want to see the old man drool on his bed in the hospital. Town was too far to go just to have dinner and going there seemed to defeat the storm.

"You better take him his teeth when you go," Mory said.

"I wonder how he's getting along without them," Hilda said. "I put them in my purse."

"You find out," Mory told her.

"All right but you'd be with us," Hilda said.

She wasn't arguing.

Twenty-Seven | Fred and Hilda changed clothes to go to town.

Fred put on a clean shirt and his best sweater, which Hilda had knitted. It was a blue cardigan with a zipper instead of buttons. His initials were stitched into the breast pocket in yellow yarn. The sweater did not fit well in the neck.

Hilda wore her red suit which had skirts. She had combed her hair and applied her makeup liberally.

Both of them were wearing galoshes.

"You sure you don't want to go?" Hilda asked Mory.

The boy was sitting in the lounger and using window light to read James Dickey's *Deliverance*. It was a fast book but when he read he had to pause frequently to rest his good eye. He was through the homosexual rape and reading eagerly.

"Ain't you going to wait for the mail after you shoveled out the mailbox?" the boy asked.

"There ain't going to be no mail," Fred said. He was leaning over Hilda's shoulder. He looked shrunken under his tweed overcoat and he had to stand on his toes to see Mory.

"There's things to warm in the icebox for your dinner, Mory," Hilda said.

Mory was planning to read Dickey for supper.

"O.K.," he said, holding his page with his thumb.

"If the lights don't come on," Fred said, "better leave us a lantern burning."

"One if by land, two if by sea," Mory said.

"Yeah. Whatever that means, do it."

"You sure you don't want to come?" Hilda said.

"Last chance," said Fred, jingling the car keys in his hand.

"See you guys later," Mory said and a feeling of relief swept over him.

When the door closed, he did not return to the book immediately. He was lost in wondering what it would be like to shoot someone with a bow and arrow. All he had to go on were Dickey's words and they excited him. They were good simple words with a crispness. Mory had actually felt the arrow strike the hillbilly but he wondered why it had not hurt. The rape hurt much more, especially when the man had to go behind the bush to wipe himself and vomit. That had been ugly enough to hurt. The arrow was much cleaner. Not as clean as a bullet might have been, if it hadn't expanded or hit bone or broken up. If it had passed through so hotly that the skin had closed up after itself. A bullet was all very clean, the boy thought, except inside afterward, when the torn heart or lung ran red in your hands. But a bullet was also easier than an arrow because it was less personal. With a bow everything had to be too right and close and personal. Dickey understood that and he saved it for the second killing in the tree, where the boy was now, when the reader rode the arrow.

Mory shrugged his shoulders and opened the book again. He decided he would never be strong enough to shoot anyone with an arrow. He couldn't even shoot a rifle perfectly at a distance. Besides he didn't want to shoot anyone yet.

Strangely Mory was not surprised when Hilda returned to the house. He didn't get out of the chair or even look up.

"We got stuck," she said. Her face said it was a crime to be stuck.

Mory had not heard them leave and he certainly hadn't heard them get stuck.

"Where?" he asked.

"There where the curve is."

"Where's Fred?"

"There. He's real angry. You don't want to go near him."

"Where you going?"

"To get sand. It's in the basement."

"How'd it happen?"

Really Mory did not care. He kept the book open.

"We got too far over and the rear wheels slipped to where it's soft."

"Can't you rock it out?"

"Fred tried that. I pushed. We just sunk deeper. He's so mad. You should see him."

"You're going to have to jack it out," Mory said. "Like in mud. With boards underneath."

"I don't want him to do that heavy work. He's sweating terrible already and he could catch a cold."

Mory closed the book and put it down.

"Wait'll I get my coat."

"I don't want you bothering yourself neither, Mory. We should have waited but Fred don't like being cooped up."

When he was ready, Mory went out to the garage for the shovel. Even after the plowing the loose snow came over his sneaker tops. The footing was slippery.

The sky had broken blue in places. Under the trees the air was cold but it was fresh.

Mory beat his mother to the car. She came slowly, sloppy in her galoshes, with the pail of sand dragging her over like a hunchback.

Fred stood by the car.

"I don't want you doing no more of that, Ma." he yelled. "I told you I'd get it."

The caretaker was already breathing in spurts and he was sweating under the overcoat. He looked like a mourner who had run all the way to the funeral of his best friend. He had removed his gloves and his hands were turning red.

The car was through the curve and headed toward the highway. The rear end was off the plowed strip and nearly into the bank. The left rear wheel was sunken to the hub and the right was slightly sunken from Fred spinning the wheels. The front end was higher, partially onto the rise at the level beginning of the driveway. The stalled car looked like a bulldog restrained from charging by a harness.

"We're going to have to jack it," Mory said.

"Just let me handle this," Fred said. He was staring at the snowbank. "I got to think."

"We'll need some boards under the rear tires."

"I wonder where I got some boards," Fred asked. "That damn Weaver threw out all them good ones of mine last summer on one of his fucking cleanups. I was saving them for something like this but he don't understand."

"Where should I put this sand?" Hilda asked.

"Just put it down, Ma. Jesus Christ, just wait and give me a chance to figure out what's best."

Mory couldn't resist asking Fred how it happened.

"Your mother was telling me something and I wasn't paying no attention. I told her to keep quiet until we got out of here. We come through the corner too wide. I couldn't see. That goddamn Schoolman didn't leave me enough room. I knew I should have checked on what he'd done before he left but I figured he'd know how to do it right. Just shows you you can't trust nobody. If he thinks I'm going to pay him for this mess, he's dumber than I give him credit for. People don't do nothing you tell them."

"You get the jack out and I'll find some boards," Mory said.

"Where you going to find them?"

"I'll find them."

"Don't you want to go to the house and warm up first, Fred?" Hilda asked.

"Jesus Christ, Hilda, I'm sweating already and you want me to go warm up. Just leave me alone and let me figure this out."

Fred kicked the bumper but not very hard.

"I knew this goddamn car was too low when I bought it, but you liked it, Ma."

Fred's hands shook as he forced them into his overcoat pockets.

When Mory came back and jacked up the left tire, there was not much clearance. He filled the hole with as many boards as he could. With his bare hands he spread sand on top of the boards and in front of both rear tires. When he lowered the car, the rear end was almost level. Mory was perspiring too and his hands were cold and filthy.

"Put it in drive," he told Fred.

"I know where to put it. Where's your mother?"

Mory pointed ahead to where Hilda was skimming loose snow from the driveway with the shovel. What she was doing was useless.

"Watch yourself, Hilda," Fred called. "If I can get moving, I ain't going to stop until I'm on the road. What you doing that for anyway? That's stupid. I told you not to do nothing."

Hilda stopped and stepped aside to watch. Mory was standing behind the car to push.

When Fred was in gear, he turned around and waved, like a bomber pilot taking off. He gave a little throttle and the wheels began to move slowly along the boards. Then he gave it more gas too sharply and the front tires spun instead of climbing and then they stopped and the rear wheels were spinning and the sand was flying and Mory could smell rubber getting hot on the wood. Fred kept tromping it and snow was flying with sand and and the rear wheels did not stop spinning until the car had swung left off the boards with the left rear fender touching the snowbank and the wheel buried even deeper than before.

Fred had to get out through the passenger door. When he did, he bumped his head on the roof and knocked his hat off into the snow. He did not bother to pick up his hat. He walked around looking at the car. It lay at a slight angle to the road and it looked sick.

"It's no fucking use," the caretaker said. "We'll have to get somebody to pull it out. I wonder why I don't do things myself when I should."

"If we had a set of chains," Mory said.

"We ain't got no chains. I tried to get him to buy me some for the truck but, aw shit, what's the difference?"

"We'll have to jack up both sides now," Mory said. He had the feeling Fred would have left if he had not said something.

The caretaker tugged at his sleeve to check his wristwatch.

"We're going to miss visiting hours anyway."

Mory jacked up both tires and set them the same way with boards and sand so they were even. Fred just watched. It was hard work in the cold and the jack didn't want to stand straight on the wet boards over the snow. Daylight was leaving the sky rapidly now and it was quite dark under the pines where they worked. Mory's trousers were damp from kneeling but he was enjoying the work. He liked to be doing it alone.

When the car came down and shook itself, Fred said, "I'm going to head her to the right a bit until I can turn them wheels and get her straightened out."

"Whatever you do, don't gun it," Mory said. He and Hilda took up their positions to push.

This time Fred accelerated more gently but, with the

front wheels turned partly against the road, the car couldn't climb out. The rear wheels began spinning before they had moved and soon they were off the boards. The car came backward until the rear wheels caught and began burying themselves even deeper in the snow. With the engine racing, the exhaust ate into the snow blackly. Fred kept his foot on the floor until Mory could see the dirt coming up below. He yelled for the old man to shut off the engine but either Fred couldn't hear him or he was enjoying the abort. The aroma of burned rubber and wood rose into the pines at both sides. Finally Hilda ran up and tapped the window. Then everything was very quiet.

"Ain't no use," Fred said, getting out slowly.

"We could work it out," Mory said.

"What's the use?"

"You want to just let it sit here?"

"It ain't that I want to," Fred said, "but it ain't going anywhere by itself."

"You're cold, Fred," Hilda said. She had retrieved her purse from the seat.

"That ain't all I am," Fred said. His hands were blue and shaking. He spun around in disgust and his head struck a tree branch. The snow was wiped smoothly into his face. Fred was really stung.

"I give up," he said. "And I'm going to cut down every goddamn one of these branches this summer. I don't care if his old lady is a fucking ecolversationalist."

"You're tired, Fred," Hilda said sadly.

Twenty-Eight | Fred coughed and that was all. The sounds came from deep within his lungs. They were harsh, moist, and lasting, almost famous.

One lantern sat on the end table. Another was in the kitchen. Most of the near light fell at Fred's stiff knees. The rest of the living room was very dark. The curtains were drawn. Hilda was half hidden in her rocker which was pushed almost to the wall near the record player. Mory sat in the corner.

The boy and his mother listened to Fred cough. They saw the shadow of him lean forward on the couch and heard it spit into the empty cereal bowl. The caretaker was holding his stomach. They had eaten chili with rice and chopped onions. Hilda had not collected the bowls so they were wherever they had put them. Fred sneezed twice and the new noise was deafening. Then he sat back again and groaned. It was as though none of them was in the same room or at least as though they were separated by great distance.

Finally Fred said, "Jesus, Ma, them onions give me heartburn."

"I'm sorry, Pa. You shouldn't have eaten them."

"I always been kind of suspicious about onions but I like their taste. I guess it don't matter now."

Fred was holding both hands into his stomach, fingers under his belt, like a truss.

"What do you mean it don't matter now?" asked Mory. The boy's voice was probing. He lay back with his feet up in the darkness.

"Folks ain't going to have to worry about old Fred too much longer."

"Please don't talk like that, Fred," Hilda said quietly.

"It's the blessed truth, ain't it? I bet I won't have to see another storm like this. I ain't worried about it. I seen enough already."

Fred held his death over their heads like a threat he might carry out. He enjoyed this power. Actually it was all he had left.

"You're just tired, is all," Hilda said.

"I'm tired myself," Mory said. He wasn't being cheerful. The room seemed to be shutting down on him and he didn't want to move.

"I ain't tired so much as beat," Fred said. "But I ain't worried. Everybody's got a light like that there lantern and they all got to run out of gas some day. I'm glad I lived when I did. Mory, you're the one that's got to live through the worst of it. You're the one that's got to worry about these low wages and inflation, this here terrible war that don't never end, them lying politicians, and all those other bad things they show you on TV."

As Fred spoke their attention was drawn to the blank television where the lantern's reflection burned like a star.

"I ain't worried," Mory said.

"No use to worry," said his mother, nodding.

"I don't know," Fred said. "I done my part. If people did a little more worrying, things could get a little better. But it don't look like the good times is coming yet. Leastways I'll never see them."

"Like you always said, Fred, we ain't starving. We ain't like some of them other people in the other countries."

"I ain't talking about starving, Ma. You can always eat grass and twigs. It's bigger things I'm thinking about now. It's like a sickness. Like the whole country was sick at once and there ain't no tonic."

"Like what?" Mory asked.

"Like, well, you take right here," Fred said. "When I first come to these lakes, they only had the logging and the guiding but there wasn't nobody couldn't find work if he bothered to look. Everybody was willing to work and there wasn't no food stamps or none of those other things that make a man insult himself if he wants to live decent. People still had the money and they wasn't afraid to spend it."

"I think," said Mory, "you can get kind of stuck where you're at."

"Yeah," said Fred, "and that ain't right."

Hilda was rocking gently. Her chair creaked.

"But there's lots of things to do," Mory said, although he wondered what they were.

"It ain't no different nowhere, Mory. And if you did something different, it'd be the same. People won't appreciate it."

"Maybe you just got to look after yourself," the boy said.

"That ain't right neither. There's too much of that already. That's the trouble. Everybody looking out for themselves."

"But when somebody looks after you, you don't like it, Fred."

Mory wasn't arguing. They were too far apart to argue.

"It ain't the same," Fred said. "In the old days you wanted to build a barn and people came over on Sunday and helped you raise it. In one day. You didn't pay them nothing. You gave them dinner is all, and if they needed help you went over and helped the next Sunday. That wasn't none of this degrading, humiliating help neither. People volunteered. You think you ever see that anymore?"

"Maybe everything's just too big to help," Mory said.

"Could be," said Fred.

"Like these governments," Hilda said. She had said nothing for a while.

"The government can't do nothing but they think they can do everything," Fred said. "Take right here. All your discussion these days is on the pollution of the environment. It's all them politicians can talk about every chance they get. So what do they do about it? Nothing. You seen it. Last summer was the first time we ever had that green scum on the whole lake. It was just crap from the public campsites.

And what do they do? They build more camps and another one of them boat launching areas down there at Back Bay and spend millions so's there can be more outboard motors and shit in the water. Even the goddamn fish is dying."

"They formed that commission," Mory said. "They're going to try to do something."

"Yeah, ass backwards. They done it themselves when they put in all them recreation parks for the nigger vote. So the niggers from New York City could come up here and crap up the area like they did their own. That was all graft and votes. You watch. They won't do nothing for the people who live here. They don't care about us."

Fred coughed again until his throat became unstuck. The sound was unpleasant and he breathed heavily around it.

"I could be making better wages," Hilda said. "Mrs. Lubin said the Maxfields would hire me to their camp and I'd only have to do sewing and laundry." Hilda shook her head to prove it. "I wouldn't have to clean no cabins. They got a maid for that."

"Yeah, that's right, Ma. You should listen to Clara. Clara Lubin's a smart woman. I always said so, even if I never cared much for Herbert. You could do it, too. Sure make old Weaver take notice. He's another who don't care. You work your ass off night and day and he don't appreciate nothing."

"At Maxfields I could get twice what he pays me," Hilda said enthusiastically. She seemed to believe herself in the darkness.

Fred's breath came in jabs.

"After all we done for him."

"I altered his trousers at least five times," Hilda said. "That was hard work on my fingers and he didn't even say thanks."

"I know, Ma. Look how Mory is always doing things for him that he don't have to."

"I don't mind," said Mory. "I think his pants are funny."

"Well, it ain't funny if you got to work on them. Why don't he just buy himself some new ones? He's got the money."

Samuel Weaver was concerned with his waistline. It was probably his first real concern about himself. In winter he added several inches to his stomach and in spring when he came to camp Hilda had to let out his favorite trousers. Gradually with exercise he lost weight and toward the end of summer he needed a belt to keep his pants up. Then Hilda would have to take them in again. This had become part of the annual camp routine, like putting in the swimming float and hauling it out again. What bothered Hilda most was that Weaver's favorite trousers were just old khakis or corduroys he had collected on his jaunts around the world to places she would never see. She followed his travels by the labels.

"I wonder what he'd do if I went to work for Maxfields?"

She spoke softly as though the idea might be dangerous.

"Probably pay you better," Fred assured her. "What could he do?"

"He don't pay me near enough for what I can do."

"I been telling you that, Ma. But you wouldn't listen."

Hilda began counting off her skills on her fingers.

"I can seamstress and I can cook. I keep his flowers and the garden. I help you and Mory outside. I wash all the windows. I look after them kids when they're too busy. I clean the camp before they get here and I put it away when they go. And I do all the laundry." At that she stopped herself sharply, as though Weaver had just entered the room.

Mory smiled. His mother's recitation sounded a lot but her work was only four months. After summer she drew unemployment and collected food stamps. When she had first gone to work for Weaver, Fred had argued for hours to complete the financial arrangements which he considered best. They had worked it out together and Weaver had agreed to pay Hilda only enough not to jeopardize the unemployment. Ever since, Fred had been trying to sabotage the deal.

"This way I don't even have no time for fishing," Hilda said. She was stretching her case.

"That's right. Weaver don't think. He'll take Mory with him to clean his fish but he don't think about us. We just got to look after ourselves, Ma. I guess we ain't important enough."

"I carry over all that mail he gets, too."

"I never seen somebody order so much stuff he don't use."

"Like them axes."

"Yeah, and all them fishing poles. I ain't even got two. He must have twenty. Reminds me to make out my spring order, Ma. Where's that new catalogue?"

Fred may have needed to cough again. He was breathing with difficulty. He sat way back on the couch. His head hung at a slight angle, as if he might drop into sleep. His big rude hands were flat on the seat beside his legs.

"He just gives us his wash," Hilda said sadly.

"What does he know?" Fred asked the lantern.

"He throws out everything you need for your work."

"He fucks up everything is what he does."

"He don't care."

"He don't know."

Mory listened to them ramble. He knew better but he wasn't saying so. It wasn't his problem.

"He don't care for us."

"He don't care for anybody. People is just objects."

"He is a millionaire," Mory said.

"Who cares?"

"Millionaires is no different. They just got the money."

"Yeah, and they ain't spending it."

"Maybe I should talk to Clara about Maxfields."

"That's right, Ma. They'd do well by you."

"What about Mr. Weaver though? He might not like it."

Mory knew his mother had just removed herself from the wage race.

"What could he do?"

"He could fire us both, Fred."

"We'd make out," Fred said, but he was lying. "Besides, I ain't got long anyway. It's you I'm worried about, Ma."

"Mory and me'd be O.K."

"Not with them other kids you got. I'd worry, Ma."

"It ain't right," Hilda said, rocking herself again.

Then very suddenly lights came on throughout the house. The television blinked and sputtered to life. There was Cary Grant, alive and well. They heard the actor begin to speak and they all sat up to listen. He might have been the president with a special message.

"Excuse me," Grant said.

"Well, look here," Fred said and he rose to lower the volume and turn off the Coleman.

Hilda had perked up straightest.

"I think I seen this one before."

"What time is it?" Fred asked, sitting down. "My heartburn's all gone, Ma."

"We'll have to reset the clock," Hilda said. She leaned

forward to inspect Cary Grant who was one of her favorites. But the movie had stopped for a commercial.

"Must be past my bedtime," Fred said. "I'll set the clock close as I can guess it. My watch is in the bedroom. Are there any of them peanuts left, Ma?"

"I think Roger ate them."

Fred stood up in the new strong light and stretched. His face was quite white.

"See," he said, "there ain't nothing. You coming to bed, Ma?"

"What you doing, Mory?"

Mory stood up. They were all together again and they could see each other. The boy didn't want to look at either of them. He started to leave the room.

"Where you going?"

"I don't know," Mory said.

"I think I'll just watch the picture a little while," Hilda said.

Twenty-Nine | Mory climbed into bed. He had opened his window wide.

He had seen stars spotting the black sky above the trees on the hill. He lay on his back and covered up.

For a while Mory was listening to the quiet. Then he was conscious of himself and he let his hands explore the smooth burns under his pajamas. He was terribly conscious of his restrictions, of his confinement. Then he was awaiting spring eagerly.

Spring came to the Adirondack lakes like a special new woman presenting herself finally. It did not come easily. There was rain first and trouble if you were too eager. Then if you were patient, the snow left the earth gradually, like clothing falling, until the ground was spotted brown in clearings, but still white in ditches and under trees where the snow stayed secretly until last. It could snow again each night on the highest peaks and in their flank gulches. The ice rose before it grayed and as it broke first along the shallow shore waters, it began to move. Roads appeared black and wet and snowbanks shrunk along the shoulders and showed brown underbellies until they too sank completely into sand.

Then there was sun to heat and dry the land in places and the snow shrank more quickly and uncollected leaves appeared like lost memories in stiff wet piles which stuck to the dirt and neither they nor the fallen pine needles would give ground yet to a rake. Then the sun burned into them and coaxed them constantly and they yielded. Trees were greening and new brown again on the mountains. Skies were very blue. And as the sun cajoled the earth more fully each day, the ice darkened and cracked into even darker veins and softened and then began to open into deep black patches at the centers of the many lakes. If there was wind, it would push the free ice onto shores and boathouse docks and onto islands, like junk collected naturally before being discarded. The air would be warm by day but the nights cool enough to halt the natural process until the next forenoon. It was a tempting time. Visiting flocks of ducks and Canadian geese selected the best open water to rest. There would be herds of them each evening and they would chatter to themselves across the last old floating ice. Sometimes they would flap their wings to their conversations or maybe rise dripping to travel five more feet to see a friend. The water fowl were great for visiting but they did not stay long. Other times there were surprises, a loon calling, a black bear along the road, prowling camps, gaunt from the long winter, his coat impossibly scruffy.

Then the ice would yield and be gone completely and

the smooth black water would rise high in the old boathouse and along the shores under the leaning yellow birches and it would be cold to touch. The days would be hot. The uncovered ground would be tousled and unkept and rough. Pale green bloom would appear on the hardwoods along the road and in the stands around the camps, lower country. The growth would be provocative and the country would be moving to a liberated rhythm. The high peaks were the last country to be moved but they could not resist and they moistened under the sun's pressure. Then there were the first bugs and the woods came alive by day and slept by night to let the frost have it's last chance. Work began again everywhere and hammers and chainsaws were broken out and their sounds permeated the forest and gave it a beat. Distances took shape and grew in the clear mountain air. It was the loveliest, freshest time to live and be alive. The sun became simply enormous as it plunged into the earth and drew it out and created smells and sounds where there had been none for too long a time.

Songbirds appeared and more of them. Trout rose in marvelous spreading circles. Squirrels got busy again. Chipmunks sprinted furiously. Raccoons were curious of everything. The does produced and displayed their fawns with a humble proud grace. There were wildflowers along the road and berry patches and absolutely everything was free to do as it pleased and the nagging torment and strict deathlike confinement of another winter was gone and forgotten like a mistaken love. And the new love held brilliant promise and proved itself faithful and lay on the earth waiting.

That was spring in Mory's mind before he slept.

Thirty | In the morning Mory dressed in dark wool. He put on a red shirt and his leather boots. The day was clear and very cold. Sun sparkled on the snow.

Fred was drinking coffee in the kitchen. Hilda had their breakfast ready when Mory sat down. Neither of them noticed his clothes.

The caretaker was in good spirits. He said something nice about Sara and he ate without complaining. The bacon was crisp. The toast was not burned and the eggs were fried right. Fred couldn't stand his eggs too greasy.

"I feel wonderful this morning," Hilda said when she had finished eating. She was wearing her bathrobe loosely and was lingering over her coffee.

"We still got that darn car," Fred said. But he didn't seem worried, as though he considered the car an old problem.

"I'll get it out for you," Mory said.

"You think you will, huh?"

"I know I will."

"What are you going to do that you didn't do yesterday?"

"Take my time," the boy said and he stood up.

"Where you going in such a rush?"

"To get your car out. You coming?"

"I'll be along," Fred said.

Outside Mory's breath was white and his ears tingled. He jacked each wheel and built a base under them from wood scraps with a long flat board on top. Once the jack slipped but the car shifted slightly away from the bank and did not leave the boards. When he lowered the last tire, the chassis cleared the boards with plenty of room. He knew they could make the road and he stood there feeling good with the cold air very sharp in his lungs until Fred came.

"You want me to drive it out?" Mory asked.

"You sure it'll go?"

Fred was dressed warmly with a scarf around his throat.

"If we take it slow and let the wheels steer themselves until we get some speed."

"I better do it," Fred said, reaching for the door.

The car started easily and Fred let the engine warm. Then he gave his pilot's wave and chose the gear. Slowly the car moved. The front wheels cleared the rise and there was enough board in the track for the rear wheels to keep the movement. Mory was pushing. The tires wanted to spin but Fred eased up without losing speed and he had traction enough to clear the rise entirely and then the car was moving hungrily toward the highway. Mory was running behind and laughing. Fred turned the car sharply to the right and brought it to rest in front of the mailbox. He got out triumphant and Mory caught up with him and they both waved at Hilda who was standing in the window.

"We did it," Fred said gladly. "I knew we would. We shouldn't have tried yesterday. It was the wrong day."

"You going to park it here?" Mory asked. The engine was still running and there were clouds of exhaust.

"I could," Fred said. "But I think I'll back into the driveway to get it off the road. You can never tell about other drivers. We might want to go to town later. I should see if I can get Bill up here this afternoon to do the job right. You done a good job, Mory."

Mory felt fine.

They collected the boards and put them back and then they went into the house for more coffee. Hilda was dressed now. They sat down at the table to listen to the Strawberry Alarm Clock Show over WNBZ. Hilda had placed a sack of sunflower seeds on the table so she would remember to feed her birds. Fred ate a few with his coffee.

They were listening to Kate Taylor sing a ballad when

Martin Findle drove up in the jeep. He carried the usual bag of newspapers into the house.

"You get stuck?" he asked. "I seen your car out there and them holes you made."

"Then you seen I got stuck, old boy," Fred said. "But I got out. I always do."

"If you'd waited, I'd pulled you out with the jeep. I didn't notice when I went by earlier or I'd of stopped."

Both men may have been grinning at each other inside.

"Where were you yesterday, old boy?"

Martin removed his glasses.

"Yesterday?" he asked, as though for him there hadn't been such a thing.

"Sure. That's when we might have needed you."

"Hell, you couldn't budge an inch in town, Fred. I ain't left the house since I seen you last. When was that? Wednesday noon, wasn't it?"

"Yep," Fred said. He was smiling now at the other caretaker.

"Well, since then, then."

"Did you lose your lights in town?"

"Nope."

"We lost them here two days."

Fred mentioned the power failure proudly, like it was a privilege.

"You know," Martin said, "I'm sure glad I got that generator at my camp. It operates on remote, you know. You don't have to do nothing with it. You should get one, Fred. Everything kept real good except for the drive. I had to go in on snowshoes this morning. But they'll be out to plow this afternoon."

Martin could not do much himself but always he had his camp perfectly under control.

"Did you have to rough it?" the other caretaker asked Mory.

"Some," the boy said. "I'm glad it didn't last any longer."

"It was quite a storm," Martin said. "I ain't seen too many worse for March."

"I have some," Fred said. "You can't never tell about this country. Turn off that darn radio, Ma."

Hilda reached over to the radio.

"Would you like coffee, Martin?"

"No thanks, Hilda. I just stopped by to see how you folks was doing. I see you look all right."

"It ain't easy," Fred said.

"I brought the papers. They tell all about the storm. Say it was bad up north of here."

"Couldn't have been no worse than here, right Mory?"

"I don't know," Mory said.

"Heard about your father, Hilda."

Martin said it kindly but he removed his glasses to wipe them so he wouldn't have to look at her.

"Thanks, Martin."

"Too bad, that. How's he getting along?"

"We don't know," she said. "We ain't been able to get a hold of him."

"How's that?"

"We're going to run in to see him this afternoon," Fred said. "We ain't had no time and we ain't been able to move too far from the door ourselves."

"Could have used the phone," Martin said casually. "Or was it out, too?"

"No, but we figured we should leave it alone for emergencies."

Fred could still think quickly on excuses.

"I see you got the snow pushed back. You get that truck of yours moving?"

"It wouldn't have done no good. Too much snow. Bill

Schoolman come by yesterday. He didn't do what I told him or we wouldn't have got stuck."

Martin nodded. "I had to give up on Bill. What was he doing here? Bring a grader, did he?"

"Looking for work, I guess. Bill's all right when he ain't drinking."

"Your folks go home, Hilda?"

Hilda didn't answer him immediately. Maybe she didn't want to reveal anything more.

Finally she said, "They left after the party."

"I heard it was some party. Too bad about your dad."

"How come you hear so much?" Fred asked. He wasn't quite annoyed with Martin yet.

The other caretaker ignored him. "I heard your dad's doing all right. Charlie Kelper's in the hospital too."

"Well, I better get to work," Fred said, pushing back from the table but not standing up.

"Yessir, quite a storm," Martin said. He enjoyed every conversation. If he had caught Fred's hint, he wasn't taking it. "I'm glad I live in town."

"You should try it out here, old boy. Be good for you. I wish we was all rich as you and could afford them town houses."

"That's right," Martin said, grinning. "Sure makes it easy. I heard most of the roads is still closed. Hard traveling yet."

"We ain't going nowhere," Fred said. "Got to work."

"Figures," Martin said.

Suddenly Hilda said, "We almost went to Florida."

"Now what you want to go do that for?" Martin asked. His eyes sparkled. "Nice as it is here? Be summer before long."

"We wasn't going anyway," Hilda said. "We was just discussing it when the lights went out."

"What could you do with them palm trees and beaches

anyway? That's for kids. Here is best for us oldsters. Right Fred? If I left, I'd die. Might die anyhow."

"Speak for yourself, old boy," Fred said. He stood up.

Martin took the hint. "Well I got to go back to town to see how the other half lives."

"We could see you later," Fred said.

"You might, if you make it."

"We'll make it. We made it out already."

"That's something," Martin said. He stood up and put on his gloves.

Fred was already heading down the hallway.

Before he left, Martin looked down at Mory and said, "I see you ain't wearing them sheets no more, Mory. Must be getting ready for something."

"I sure don't know what," Mory said.

Hilda opened the door. When she closed it, she said, "You did change your clothes, didn't you?"

"He go yet?" Fred yelled from the bathroom. "Jesus, he's a nosy bastard."

Thirty-One | The mail came and Hilda walked out to collect it. Except for some fishing catalogues it was junk.

Fred picked over each piece before tossing it away. Then he looked up and said, "Hey, let's go to town. There ain't nothing here."

"What do we need?" Hilda asked.

"To get out of here most," Fred told her.

"You sure we can leave?"

"Hilda, will you listen to me?"

It did not take any of them long to get ready.

Fred drove with Hilda perched beside him. He was

whistling and he laughed as he swerved the car deliberately on the snowy road to scare her. He was sure of himself.

Mory had the back seat.

When they saw a car stuck in the road ahead, the caretaker stopped his foolishness. Two women stood beside the car. They were wearing overcoats and they began waving when they heard the other car. Fred slid over into the left lane but he did not slow down.

"We going to stop?" Mory asked.

"Can't," Fred said. "What can we do for them?"

"Nothing," Hilda said. She was clutching her father's teeth and she began laughing.

"We could see if they need help," Mory said.

"It's their own fault. What can they do for us?"

"Nothing," Hilda said again. She was still laughing.

"That's right," Fred said and he roared past the two women and onto the wider road which bypassed the fish hatchery.

Mory turned around. The women were showered with snow. They were brushing themselves off. He felt sorry for them and he hated his mother's laugh.

"We should have stopped," Mory said softly.

"We should do alot of things," Fred said. He turned his neck to look at the boy. He was grinning and Mory hated him, too.

"But we can't, Mory old boy. We can only do things we got to do. Sometimes we can't even do them."

Mory looked ahead between his mother and Fred and saw the bald white crown of Whiteface. He thought the top of the mountain seemed to be floating above the forest. The mountain was way up there today and he realized it would be always. Then he felt Fred give the car more gas and he saw the snowbanks fly by on each side. Whiteface slipped behind the trees of the Forest Home Road turn and the car entered the curve toward Lake Clear.

They were rolling again now beautifully. They drove right past the hospital, forgetting to stop in their rush to get to the supermarket.

The evening did not go well. The water was high in the river outside the window of the restaurant where they ate. The ducks were dirty and cold and they did not look happy. The steaks came with garlic bread and watery mushrooms that looked uncomfortable like the ducks in the river. The steaks were underdone but there wasn't time to send them back before the movie. Their fingers glistened from the bread and the garlic taste was with them forever. The restaurant was out of Fred's favorite steak sauce so he could complain about that, too.

Mory ate without complaining. To him the meal was decent. It was good to be out of the house for the evening. He forgot about the two women on the road who had discouraged him and made him hate.

Hilda was embarrassed by Fred's complaints. It was supposed to be a good time. She ate without speaking, except to mention the poor salad dressing. It was like her to pick on something nobody else had noticed and to object mildly.

The caretaker was happier over coffee but later the movie presented alot of violence and a sad ending without redeeming social value except as an accurate slice of life shoved up ahead of the audience boldly. The movie infuriated Fred because he had paid for it like the unsatisfactory dinner and because he had to walk past all the town children waiting for the second show when he left the theatre.

Going home Fred was tense, as if it were snowing again in his mind and this time wouldn't stop.

"We ain't going to no more movies, Ma," he said. "Leastways I ain't. If they don't come over the TV, that's too bad. We don't see them."

"What about John Wayne?"

"What about him? He comes on the TV sometimes. We see him enough."

"Maybe something you could like will come to the drive-in later, Fred."

"I ain't going there no more either. How can you tell what you like, anyway? It's all so different anymore when you go see it. Like that thing tonight. Anyhow we'll be going fishing again, Ma. Then things'll be all right."

"First we've got to get all that raking done when we can see the ground," Mory said. He was huddled in the back seat. He wasn't getting enough heat from up front.

"What's your rush?" Fred asked. "I think we'll do a little fishing first. Before we get to them leaves, right Ma? Soon as the ice goes out we'll go back there to our favorite pond."

They did have a favorite pond which was close to the camp. They could always catch bullheads and a few trout there after dark. They used the pond when they didn't want Weaver to know where they were. But unlike the boathouse on the big lake, it was very buggy.

"I could eat a fresh trout as soon as you catch him, Pa."

"Sure be better than them steaks we had tonight. I don't know what's the matter with that place, or why people go there, neither. It never was much good."

"I don't know who's cooking in there now," Hilda said.

"It's Jeff Bates," Mory said.

"Yeah, how do you know?"

"I saw him."

"It figures," Fred said. "Bates ain't no cook."

"He never was no cook," Hilda said. "He always used to work for the phone company."

"Yeah, ain't that something? Maybe the real cook's over on some switchboard. We should have gone to Howard

Johnson's for them fried clams. You like them clams, Ma."

"I do, too," Hilda said. "Sometimes."

"I enjoy Dew Drop's," Mory said.

"You always did, Mory," Hilda said.

"He don't care what he eats as long as he's eating, isn't that right, Mory?"

"Isn't what right?"

"You don't care what you eat. You don't even care what you do."

"Oh, he does, too, Pa. Mory used to do alot."

"I could do things," Mory said.

"But you don't care. That's what I'm saying."

Hilda nearly turned around to look at Mory. She was sitting sideways across the front seat but she was watching the road. She wouldn't have seen Mory in the dark. The road was slick in places and the tires crunched on the packed snow where it was turning to ice. Fred was hunched over the wheel.

They crossed the tracks too fast at Lake Clear and the car lurched a bit. It startled Fred enough for him to mutter something. When they passed the Malone intersection he stepped on it. They were flying and full of release, bearing down. The night air was very dark outside. They could almost see the cold in the headlamps as they sliced through it.

Mory could tell his mother was nervous. He knew she wanted to say something to the caretaker about the way he was driving but he also knew she wouldn't. She would just hold on until they made it. Hilda could care very much about certain things but she wouldn't let her caring influence what she did. Fred was right about Mory though. He just didn't care. Now he looked out the window. There wasn't much light on the side. He felt the black glass with his fingertips and it was cold. He realized the evening had been a bust. He felt awfully dark and unsatisfactory about it. That didn't make him care any more but it made him want to do something. The car slowed at the tennis court. The light in the house was the best part of the night.

"I'm damn glad that's over," Fred said, turning into the drive.

"We didn't even go see Pa, did we?" Hilda asked.

"How'd we forget that?"

"We was too eager to enjoy ourselves."

"But we got the groceries, didn't we? I hope they ain't froze."

"We should at least have left off his teeth."

"Grandpa'll last," Fred said, driving into the garage.

The air was cold on their faces when they walked between the garage and the house with the grocery sacks. There were no stars. Fred stomped his boots too many times before going in.

Mory went into his room and hung up his jacket. When he came back to the kitchen, Fred was sitting at the table. He was looking over at the telephone as though it might ring and save him from something the rest of them wouldn't understand. The windowpanes were growing frost. The caretaker had taken off his overcoat and thrown it in the living room but he still wore his galoshes. He removed his glasses and rubbed his tired eyes.

"I can't stand to waste time like that," he said. "I wonder why nothing works out the way you think it will?"

"It don't seem to, does it, Fred?" Hilda asked.

"That's what I was saying. I bet it's going to snow again tomorrow."

"Maybe it won't," Hilda said.

"You see that sky?"

"I couldn't see anything. It was so dark and you was going so fast."

Fred looked at her without his glasses. Mory wondered what he could see.

"I got you home, didn't I?" the caretaker asked.

"Sure, Pa."

"Well, what's the problem?"

"There's no problem."

"Well, don't say nothing if you ain't got no problem. Pour me a glass of milk, Ma, and fix me a ham sandwich. I'm hungry and that movie got me all screwed up so I won't be able to sleep."

"Did it scare you, Pa?"

"Just fix me a sandwich, would you? I don't like that kind of movie, is all. No, it didn't scare me."

"It scared me," Hilda said. "You want a sandwich, too, Mory?"

"No," the boy said. He sat down under the telephone.

Fred did not put on his glasses. His nose looked larger and his boots were dripping water on the floor.

Hilda poured the glass of milk and stood it on the table in front of the caretaker. Then she got out the fixings and went to the sink to make the sandwich.

Mory was thinking he didn't want his mother to make the sandwich. He was caring about it. It was such a simple thing for her to be doing but he didn't want her to do it, not now, not anymore or ever. While Mory was thinking this he was seeing the shotgun in the corner like a forgotten promise. He was touching the barrel without moving and taking the gun out coldly in his hands and pointing it at Fred's left ear just behind the bleary old eye. The explosion he alone heard rocked the house like the daily supersonic fighters from Plattsburgh, only closer. He could see most of the right side of Fred's face wind up in the sink and on the cabinets.

Mory saw his mother turning around bewildered in time to watch the remains of Fred reach the floor. She always reacted imprecisely. He heard Fred thumping and

Hilda dropping the ham knife and then the crash of the shotgun when he dropped it.

Mory was bent over with his eyes shut.

He heard Hilda hold something back in her throat and say, "Mory, look what you done."

"He did it. He made me do it."

"Oh, God, Mory, we got to do something now. We can't run and we can't fix it."

He knew when his mother realized part of her husband's head was on her sleeve, she would begin to pick it off in pieces. She would start crying. She would be shaking violently when she came over to Mory. She would almost sit down on his lap but catch herself and kneel and put her arm around him. She would look back at Fred slowly and stare at his black rubber boots and the red puddle of blood from the top of his neck. She would look at the caretaker for a long time as though she expected him to rise again or start smelling.

"Why'd you have to do that, Mory? We could have made it better. Was it so bad?"

"No. I don't care."

"What were you thinking of to make you do that?"

He could see her reaching up for the telephone, fumbling and nearly dropping the receiver. For a second Mory realized his mother would never do anything right.

"What are you doing?"

"I'm going to call Martin to help. What were you thinking, Mory?"

Mory was numb. He knew he could do it which almost made it better than having done it, except it solved nothing.

"What were you thinking, Mory?"

Fred belched uncomfortably on the ham sandwich and dropped his hands to adjust his belt. Moist bread was stuck to his gums. Hilda stood next to him, very tired, nearly swaying, but waiting for his plate and milk glass.

"Nothing," Mory said. He stood up and bumped his head on the telephone.

"Watch your head," Fred said, smiling before he belched again louder. "What's the matter with him?"

"I seen you thinking, Mory."

"Maybe I was thinking of the lilacs," Mory said, standing quite still.

"Is that right?" his mother asked, taking the plate from Fred.

THE WORST THING

"Tell me the worst thing you know about Larry," Gene McKelvey asked Bill Muson seriously.

"I have heard some things," Bill said. "But I don't know what's worst."

They were shoveling the snow off Larry Grenley's roof. During the last three days, two feet had fallen and according to the radio, more was on the way. Yesterday some of the snow had started to melt but it had frozen up again during the night. Now there were very big icicles along the edge of the roof and a leak in Larry's living room.

"One is he don't shovel his own snow," Bill said.

"That ain't bad," said Gene. "I heard his back's poor."

"I seen him work with his back."

"Then tell me something else you heard."

"They say he's got it going strong with Bud Purdy's wife."

"That's done with and over," Gene said.

"That was pretty bad though."

"Can't say I blame him, Bill. I looked at her a time or two myself."

"Nothing wrong with looking. At least he ain't got no drinking problem."

"He drinks enough though."

"No worse than others, Gene."

"Try again," Gene said, shoveling. They were both dressed warmly and he was sweating underneath.

"I can't think of nothing," Bill said. "He's got a good family that stays together. Probably better than ours."

"You ain't trying hard enough, Bill."

"Just don't know nothing bad about him. That is, nothing that really couldn't be said about you or me."

Gene stopped shoveling and he rested on the handle. To the east he saw Whiteface. The big mountain was clear, topped with the new snow, very white against the cold blue sky.

"Must be something," Bill said, working toward the middle of the roof and having to throw the snow wide to get it out over the edge.

"Must be," Gene said.

"Why'd you ask me anyway?"

"Figured you'd know."

"Kind of stupid," Bill said. "To be looking for the worst in a man."

"When you can't find it," Gene said.

"I know something," Bill said. He stopped working to light a cigarette. "He don't never buy nobody a drink."

"But you just heard him say he'd give us one when we was through," Gene said.

"Yep, he did say that," Bill said, and he threw away the cigarette.

"You know, Bill," Gene said, "Larry does still drive one of them Kaiser cars."

"Hey, Gene," Bill said, "let's hurry up and finish this roof so's we can have that drink."

"Yep," said Gene, shoveling again. "Let's get her done."

They were just two old men shoveling Larry Grenley's roof. They just couldn't think of the worst thing about him.

THEY'LL TAKE FLIES

———◆◆◆———

Frank Laser tripped coming through the door but recovered nicely.

"Well look who's here and what he's doing to himself," Clara Petoe said from behind the bar.

"Never liked that fool step," Frank said, walking up to her. "I think I'll axe it out."

"It's supposed to slow you down, Frank."

"It works," said Frank. "Hello, Clara."

"Look what the cat dragged in," said the woman, chuckling now and shaking hands. "How you been doing, Frank?"

Frank shook hands across the bar and took the stool nearest the television. The set was off. It received only one station from Plattsburgh and there was nothing worth watching at noon.

"Doing pretty good," Frank said.

"Going up to camp now, are you?"

"Been and going again."

"That's fine, Frank," said Clara. "You'll have real good weather."

The day was full of sunshine. Already there was a taste of summer in the Adirondack air. In less than a month there would be black flies and tourists at all accessible lakes. Clara had installed her screen door at the front of the bar but inside it was dark and cool with the old smells of winter lingering. There were no tourists yet inside. No one else besides Frank was at the bar.

"You had a good winter?" Frank asked the woman.

"Very poor, Frank," she said. "It was very long. One of these winters I really will close."

"Now how many times have I heard that?"

"One of these years you'll be hearing the last of it," Clara said.

Frank looked the woman over without staring. He was seeing one of the northcountry's permanent fixtures. Clara was in her late sixties and she could remember every minute of her years from horse to buggy to Cadillac. She could talk about them.

Frank saw she hadn't changed during the long winter. She hadn't gained much weight. Her gray hair was only slightly bluer and her face may have acquired a couple more wrinkles. She still wore the same red sweater for tending bar and the same spectacles with the green elastic band that went around her neck.

"You still drinking your old fixer?" she asked.

"Might as well," Frank said.

"Did you hear about Lou?"

"Nope," he said, knowing he would. "Not yet."

"He's gone," Clara said, turning around to reach his bottle on the shelf.

The price of a shot was written on the label of each bottle. Frank's whiskey was in the cheap section.

"Where'd he go this time?" Frank asked, remembering Lou Fisher was apt to leave his wife now and then. Their relationship was well known at Clara's bar and not uncommon in this country. Lou always came back.

"He passed," Clara said, turning to face him with the bottle.

"I hadn't heard," Frank said and he rubbed his jaw like he'd been punished.

Frank hadn't shaved for three days. The fishing had been excellent and he felt to shave would ruin his luck. Now he felt the new beard on his chin and he decided he wouldn't tell Clara how many fish he had outside in the car.

"I'm sorry to hear that about Lou," he said.

"Yes, it was very sad," Clara said. She put two ice cubes into a glass and measured the full shot of Frank's whiskey before pouring it over the ice. She finished the drink with plain water from the type of plastic jug made for mixing frozen orange juice. There was nothing fancy about either Clara or her place.

She gave the drink to Frank and said, "You going to have a chaser?"

"Nope," said Frank, watching her again as she folded her arms across her big chest and leaned back against the shelf that held the bottles. He saw she was watching him too.

"She done it, Frank," Clara said.

"Who done what?"

"His wife, that's who. She done it."

"You mean she killed him?"

"She might as well have," Clara said with the finality of a judge giving his verdict. "Her chasing around all the time and him having to work. Him having to be both father and mother to them kids. That's just what it came down to."

Frank sipped his drink. He wondered if he smelled of fish.

"I didn't know Lou well," he said.

"Lou was a very nice man. That's the pity of it."

"I had a problem of my own like that once."

"I know you did."

"I settled it," Frank said. Then he said, "Clara you must know everything."

"For all the good it does me, I guess I do," the woman said, smiling slightly.

"I guess that's right, too," Frank said.

"Yes," said the woman slowly, "for all the good it does me."

"I liked what I saw of Lou," Frank said, noticing for the first time how Clara's hair seemed to be growing in clumps. He had never noticed that before about her hair and he was briefly fascinated.

Clara put a hand to her head and said, "Lou was a wonderful person. She didn't deserve him. She just broke his heart. And him working so hard to please her."

"Must have been rough. What'd he do for work anyway?"

"State. Surveying mostly. Some plowing in the winter. Lou was a smart man and he worked hard."

Frank sipped the drink and said, "One night in here he gave me a poem he'd written. He'd put it down in longhand on ordinary paper. It looked like fancy scribing but I never did read it."

"What'd you do with it?"

"Threw it away probably. I'm sure I didn't know what to do with a poem."

Clara laughed gently and said, "I never knew Lou was a poet."

"I don't think he was," said Frank, drinking.

"Just imagine Lou Fisher being a poet," Clara said. "That's a good one."

"How many kids did he leave?"

"Only the four. Now she'll have to stay home once in a while. Of course, Ralph Bigelow's already moved in with her. He didn't waste a minute. Ralph's the latest, you know. He was there when Lou died."

"I don't like to hear that."

"Me neither."

"Is Ralph the one that works the gravel pit? I can't quite place Ralph."

"That ain't all," said Clara. She hoisted her apron and walked around the end of the bar to the nickelodeon. Without hesitation she plugged a Jim Reeves tune. Then she came back and said about the singer, "He has such a nice voice."

"He's dead too," Frank said.

"It was a terrible thing. He was too young to be dead."

"Which one?"

"Lou Fisher," she said. "Want another?"

"Nope," said Frank. "One's the limit today."

"Folks say Lou came home after work and found her with Ralph. Of course, he must have known what she was up to all along. If he didn't, he was the only one from here to Malone who didn't. All the kids knew."

"Did he hit Ralph?" Frank asked, without knowing why.

"You know Lou wouldn't hit nobody. He wasn't like that. Maybe poets ain't supposed to hit nobody."

"What'd he do though, Clara? How'd he act?"

"They say he just stomped out into the yard and keeled over by the pickup. They say she and Ralph stayed inside and finished whatever they was doing. They didn't find Lou until Ralph decided it was time for him to go."

"What'd Ralph do then, Clara? Lou must have been pretty near froze up."

"They say he put Lou in the back of the pickup and took him to town. That part was in the paper. Of course, he was dead then and there was nothing anybody could do. But do you know, they say she rode up front with Ralph, just like they was going to the drive-in picture show? She never showed no grief or nothing. I swear I don't know what that woman sees in Ralph. The other way around, too."

"It sounds like bad business," Frank said, rising off the stool.

"Don't it?" Clara said. "They only buried Lou a week

ago. They waited for the thaw. I guess there's been quite alot of insurance money that Lou left."

Frank looked at the woman and said, "Well, I got to get going, Clara. I got to get to work."

Clara laughed and said, "Are you working, Frank? You're not working. I bet them fish are real hard work."

"Now, come on," Frank said, paying for the drink. "I told Bill Jenvy I'd help him rake at Tennyson's camp."

"A man can't fish all the time but you smell like you been doing it," Clara said.

"Bill says the Tennysons are coming early so you'll probably see them before long."

"That's nice," Clara said. "The Tennysons are wonderful people. They always send me a Christmas card."

"Keep me informed, will you, Clara?" Frank said.

"If you stop by," the woman said. "You know I just never knew that Lou Fisher was any kind of a poet."

SWEARING OFF

―◄●►―

"Holy shit, do I hate April," Danny Muldoon said. He stepped on the pedal to change gears, then changed his mind. As the clutch caught again, the old White dump truck sighed and shook. The truck had been painted green but now it looked sick.

Bob Waite sat across the double sticks from Danny. He was looking at the road which was damp in places. He was tired and his arms ached from shoveling.

"Never much of a month is it?"

"I mean it's nothing, Bob," Danny said. "It's too late for more winter but it's too goddamn early for spring."

"Around here," Bob said, still watching the road but rubbing his chin slowly.

"Well, where you think I'm talking about? Mexico or someplace?"

"I been other places," Bob said.

They started downhill and Danny had to concentrate. He used both hands. Without a muffler the noise was terrible. The White had a load of manure and they were losing some of it to the road. When they reached the bottom and began to climb again, Danny relaxed, as though he had done something dangerous.

"No spring this year," he said. "Only summer, whenever it decides to get here. And not much of that, I bet."

"Today's a nice day," Bob said.

"Sure, for once. But how many we had?"

Danny looked over for an answer that never came.

"It's good to be able to ride with the windows down though, ain't it?"

"Yeah, sure, it's nice."

Bob looked at the snowbanks slumping along the road shoulder. They were dirty with sand. The winter had been rough and Bob remembered the plows. There had been a lot of plowing.

"Where we going anyway?" Danny asked. Now he was leaning forward against the steering wheel while the dump truck struggled to make the last hill before town. Near the top, the sun struck the steel radiator grill so he put on his sunglasses.

"The Rest A-Bit," Bob said.

"What the hell's that? Drive-in or flophouse?"

"Motel."

"Same thing," Danny said. "Only you got to take your own." He looked at Bob again and seemed about to laugh. His hair was sticking straight out in spots as though he had just gotten up. With his mouth open part way and the cheap crooked sunglasses, he looked funny.

"You know which motel it is?"

"Sure."

"I don't think I do. I don't think I ever used it."

"They changed the name. It's fancy Triple-A. They probably wouldn't let you in."

"Maybe not in daylight," Danny said seriously and he chuckled. "I've used most of them though. What they want this goddamn shit for?"

"Lawn. Harry said they're going to rebuild a lawn."

"Yeah? Harry must know. Lots of luck, folks. Little early, ain't it?"

"Maybe."

"They can have it, and they'll sure get it. Hey, you want a smoke, Bob?"

Bob looked down at Danny's Luckies propped in the open ashtray on the dash. He could taste one lit.

"I got to quit," he said.

"What you want to quit for?"

"I been watching them new ads and I didn't like it."

"Don't they make you feel rough? They make you feel guilty of something. Like you was destroying yourself. Look though, when I'm driving like this, I don't got to smoke. I can leave them lay there. When I'm taking it easy, that's when I need them."

"When you quit them," Bob said slowly, "you'll need them all the time."

They topped the hill and picked up speed for the two mile straight to town. Snow was everywhere. The trees were bare. Danny toed the gas pedal.

Then Bob said sharply, "You better watch it. There's cops at the intersection." He pointed through the windshield at two black and white New York State patrol cars on each side of the road.

Danny grunted and said, "You can tell it'll be spring soon if them bastards are out. Like a bunch of fucking black flies."

"What they want to start so early for?"

"I don't know. You know?"

"I don't know," Bob said.

"Maybe they got quotas to fill every month," Danny said. "But this just looks like a check. Sure hope they don't check us. Not without a muffler."

"They're stopping them going the other way," Bob said. He watched the troopers grow. They were standing in the road, flagging traffic. They waved as Danny drove by.

"But we got to go back through them," Danny said

relaxing. "They'll get us, too. I don't even know if we got taillights on this rig. What's the matter with fucking Harry anyway?"

"He quit chauffeuring."

"It's his stuff though. He ain't too big to pay the fine. All I do is drive. That's what I'm going to tell them. Tell them to damn well goose the boss if they got complaints."

They began passing a lake on Bob's side. The lake was still frozen but Bob could see gray ice out in the middle.

"Starting to water up," he said.

Danny lit a cigarette and exhaled out the window. The new hospital was on his side.

"Been a shit funny winter," he said. "Now it's breaking up from the bottom. Warm wind'll blow it out of here. You watch."

Bob nodded very gradually, as though to nod were the only move he had strength left to make. He was glad they could dump the manure and leave. They couldn't pay him enough to spread it today.

"I stayed off the lakes this winter," he said. "I bet I didn't run my machine ten times. There was a layer of water always under the top of the ice. You may not have drowned but you'd have damn sure gone through."

"So I heard," Danny said, braking now to meet the town limits. The truck backed off seven times. At the slower speed the sunny air was warmer in the cab.

"Shit, the old sap's going to run," Danny said, stretching both arms without letting go of the wheel. "And I ain't talking about maple syrup."

Bob read the billboard of club notices. He read them every time he passed, like another warning.

"You want to get married, Bob, quick as you can. You're missing the best thing there is. You're missing the only thing."

"I ain't missing it," Bob said. "I get it when I can. I just ain't getting it so regular."

"I can't live without it. I got a good wife. You know my wife, don't you?"

"I seen her," Bob said. "She's good looking."

"She's just a kid, really. She didn't know nothing when we got married. At first I had to show her everything. Like dropping down. Now she shows me. She's been reading this book. Like this morning. Right on the goddamn kitchen table. I hadn't even finished my coffee. She says the book says do it wherever you feel like it." Danny began to chuckle. "God, it tickled me."

"That's showing you," Bob said, laughing too. He saw where the warehouse had burned in January. Nothing was left except charred white lumber and a pile of broken windows. He had gotten to the fire too late to help but nothing had been saved.

"I swear I can't understand you," Danny said. "There's half a dozen girls in this town who'd go naked in the street to marry you."

Bob didn't answer.

"If I were you, I'd fuck them all and then make up my mind. Sort of give them each a tryout."

"I can't stand their bullshit," Bob said.

"That don't have nothing to do with fucking."

"But I can't stand it after. It's like I always got to come up for air. They suffocate me. I'm like a damn fish out of water. Maybe I'm not ready for that just yet."

"Shit, marriage ain't dying," Danny said. "You just got to breathe deeper. You know, Bob, maybe you got one of them hangups."

When they stopped for the traffic light at the edge of the business district, Danny honked the horn at a thin young girl crossing the street. She was wearing shorts and her legs were thin and very white. She stopped and looked at them, trying to seem annoyed. Danny honked again and Bob looked quickly into the hotel window.

"I can look, can't I?" Danny asked.

"You can do whatever you want," Bob told him.

"I do, too," Danny said and he started up again under the green light. He stayed in low gear and the exhaust barked at the buildings.

"So I heard," Bob said, raising his voice over the noise.

Each time they passed a girl, Danny either honked or waved wildly. Or else he asked Bob if he wanted her, as though he were the town's provider. He was having fun. With the fine warm day, like a surprise, there were lots of girls out walking. It almost seemed like spring.

"So you heard, huh?" Danny said and he pulled the horn again. "You want that one?"

"Later," Bob said.

"You ought to get married, Bob. Be much better off."

"Yeah, they ought to open a whorehouse around here, too."

"I'd run it."

"You and your wife."

"Now that's an idea. I could look, couldn't I?"

"Sure, Dan," Bob said softly, as though now he might be avoiding a fight.

"It would damn sure save a lot of these young lovelies walking around pushing carriages."

Bob was looking at the girls now and thinking everything about them.

"I hope none of these new kids is mine," Danny said.

At the other end of town there was a second light and they had to stop again. When they started turning left, they passed a pickup which was slowing down. Danny honked at the driver who was young like them. His greasy black hair shone in the sun and his cigarette pack was rolled up in the sleeve of his T-shirt.

"Who was that?" Bob asked because he'd missed him.

"That worthless fucker," Danny said, timing his words to match the throw of the shift. "Him and me used to run around together. We was buddies when I worked at the hotel in Placid. I got arrested with him for running a whorehouse."

"I must have missed that," Bob said. "Say again."

"Yeah, for running a whorehouse. For what you just said this town needs. Only I wasn't really."

"What were you doing really?"

"What do you think?"

"It's kind of hard to make a mistake on a thing like that."

Bob was prepared to hear anything from Danny.

"I had this room, see? Anybody could come up there if they brought a sixpack. The landlord lived on the same floor and he knew what was going on. One night these two girls and that guy back there and me was sitting around naked. We were bareassed but we were just sitting around talking and joking and drinking a little beer. I had to go take this piss and I put on a pair of scivvies to go down the hall. When I come back there's a knock on the door and the guy outside says it's the police. So I figure he's just another of my buddies playing games and I told him to come on in. They do and it's the cops."

Bob began to laugh. He almost reached for a cigarette. "What gave?"

"I did. They took me and that guy down and booked us for running a whorehouse. We had to spend the night in jail. When the girls got dressed they came down to visit. The cops loved it. They let the girls come in back and everything. They all knew me anyhow. The charges were dropped but that skunk landlord threw me out. I lost two months' rent paid in advance."

"Was he the guy who blew the whistle?"

"Hell no. One of the girls told her parents where she was going nights."

"Man, you must have been a lousy."

"I was," Danny said, working the truck carefully around some deep chuckholes that were filled with water. "Welcome to the Ho Chi Minh Trail," he said.

Here there was lots of water in the street from melting snow and another lake to the right. This lake was partially open and the water looked dark and cold against the remaining ice. Some of the ice may have been floating. On the other side a few lawns were bare.

They passed a trailer truck loaded with green canoes and Bob said, "I wonder where he thinks he's going?"

"Probably trying to find Florida," Danny said.

Bob said, "I'd like to get me another canoe. What I'd really like to have is one of them old guideboats."

Danny didn't seem to hear.

"Yeah," he said, "every night after work we had a table reserved over at Freddie's. They don't usually reserve for anybody but they knew we'd come. We'd fill it, too. When the cops came in on a bust, they left us alone. They knew I wasn't legal."

"You must have been bad."

"Not really, but after that whorehouse charge, I figured I better quit fucking around. That's when I first thought about getting married. I mean seriously. I mean I knew I couldn't live without it. You get kind of spoiled. That's what you ought to do, Bob."

"I ain't even talked to the right one yet."

"Try them all."

"Much less tried her."

"If it was me again," Danny said, "I think I'd go get me an Oriental. Was you ever in on any of that stuff?"

"I was stationed in Germany for a while," Bob said.

"That's good stuff too, but this is different. This is the

whipped cream of snatch. This is why they call snatch, snatch, see? I mean it can just reach out and grab you like it had claws. Most of them ain't got a hell of a big chest on them but what they got hiding down where it counts makes up for everything else. Man it's like a dream."

"You should be getting close to the Rest-A-Bit," Bob said. They were nearly through town.

"I had this broad in Japan that wanted to marry me. I told her, 'Sorry Babe, I got me a brand new wife in the States.' You know what she says? She says, 'That O.K., Joe, can have your wife there and me here.' Now that's a damn nice way of looking at things, ain't it?"

Bob nodded.

"Damn right," Danny said. "I told her, 'I got you here already.' Shit, my wife would have killed me."

A girl in jeans was walking ahead on the road. Her pants were tight. When they approached, Danny slowed down. He timed it perfectly so the right front tire would splash her with filthy cold water from a huge chuckhole. At the last moment he had to swerve the truck to catch it and he did. The girl got soaked. Bob got the dirty look.

"You've got to be a real bastard, Danny."

"Jesus, yes. I know that one, pal. She's married."

Danny reached for another cigarette.

"You want one?" he asked.

"Sure," Bob said, taking the pack.

AT THE LAKES THEN

In those days summer folks began coming to River Junction about the end of June. Most of them cleared out by Labor Day. That way they missed the black flies early and the first cold weather late.

I remember being told most of them came from New York and Philadelphia and some from Boston. I know they came in cars and planes, sometimes their own planes, and, of course, on the train while it still ran passengers. That train was long and slow and it stopped at the Junction every day to let off summer folks and mail sacks.

Most summer folks had fine big camps on the lakes. I remember hearing how they always had more servants than family or friends staying at their camps and how mostly the owners never did nothing except to entertain, or go to parties across the lakes in their motorboats, or maybe get up a little inner strength to climb a low mountain that we could run up, or maybe catch a trout on a fly where the water was stocked recently, or go sailing. They did just about nothing all summer because they could afford to.

We never did none of them things. We never did no sailing. We drank a little beer and fished nights with crawler worms. All we ever had was an old guideboat that we'd use for fishing when we had the time. Everybody up there on those lakes knew all a guideboat had for sails or a motor was a pair of oars and the hands around them.

In those days my Uncle Bart used to tell me, "You better pull them oars, Sonny, or you ain't going nowhere."

I'd get mad at him but I guess he was right all along or I wouldn't be here now where I can't get back.

THE ROADHOUSE
RADICAL

"Harry, I need another beer and let's have one for Mike," Fred Monrovey told the bartender.

Harry nodded and opened two more bottles of Utica Club. He set them on the bar in front of Fred and Michael Canby.

The evening was barely kicking but Fred had been drinking since getting off work at four. He worked construction. He had a wife and five children and he did not mind working nights. The job kept him in shape so his drinking did not hurt a thing. Already he was slightly drunk.

"Thanks, Fred," Mike said. "I'll handle the next round."

"I got a pretty good joke," said Fred, pouring the fresh beer into his glass on top of what remained of the old one.

"Let's hear it," Mike said.

"You know how to solve this population problem they're always talking about?"

"Castrate people like you."

"No, Christ," said Fred. "This is a joke I'm telling you."

Mike poured his beer and said, "O.K., but it better be good. Swing away."

Harry had moved closer.

"It's simple," said Fred, taking a sip and wiping a crusty hand over his mouth.

He swallowed and said, "You take all the chinks and coons and put them together and call them chiggers. Then you spray for them."

Harry laughed before Mike. Then they were all laughing. Mike was forcing himself to laugh. Then he and Fred were drinking the fresh beer.

Mike was the tennis assistant at the local club. He lived in Florida but he had spent the better part of the last year in the Adirondack resort town. He had done odd jobs like teaching tennis. He was in his early twenties and his brown hair was crew cut. Although he was tan and very athletic, he considered himself neither handsome nor a professional tennis player. Nor was he a member of the club where he taught. He did most of his carousing here.

"What are you going to do now the club's about closed?" Fred asked. He had gotten over his joke. This was the Labor Day weekend and most of the club's facilities would be shutting down until ski season began.

"Take a vacation," Mike said.

"You don't need no vacation," Fred said. "Where you going?"

"Nowhere."

"You mean just stick around like some old lady and watch the leaves turn color?"

A smirk spread across Fred's worn face. "I sure wish I could take that kind of vacation."

"You can, Fred. You should just take one. Buy yourself a dress."

"Can't do it."

"Sure you can."

"Can't either. Got to work. Winter be here before you and I both know it. Don't have no time for vacations."

Fred was nodding his head above his glass as he struck each point.

"You ought to just get up and go," Mike told him.

"Can't do it. Schools are open next week. The snow could lay me off. I'm working nights now."

Again his head was bobbing.

"You're not working tonight."

"Nope, not tonight," Fred said. "I got to have some time off. I ain't had no vacation since I was married. Don't have no time. Don't have time for tennis neither. You know how it is."

"O.K.," said Mike.

"Going to play a pretty song now," Fred said. He rose from the barstool, using both hands to support himself. He put on his orange hunting cap and he was swaying slightly when he went to plug the jukebox.

Mike watched him weave across the scuffed floor. He jerked to a stop at the machine and leaned on it to make his selection. A Don Messer tune flooded the barroom. There was no traffic on the highway outside the bar and the screen door was closed. Mike heard the fiddles clearly. He continued to watch Fred as the burly construction worker began a jigstep, balancing with his hands, making his way back to the bar.

Fred spun the top of the stool and then sat down to stop it.

"Yessir," he said, "that's the kind of tune can make a man cry if he's drunk enough."

"Don't cry, Fred," Mike said.

He was going to add something but the bar door swung open. They both turned to watch twelve young persons enter the room, one right after the other, in line, like a column of tanks.

"Jesus Christ," said Fred. "What's this? An invasion?"

"Kids," said Harry.

"From the lake," said Mike. He was watching them enter. It was like a parade.

Mike knew most of them. Mostly they were sons,

daughters, and guests of people who owned summer camps around the nearby lake. Most of them he had seen at the club and all of them looked expensive.

"Oil up the register, Harry," Fred told the bartender.

"I'm ready," Harry said, like a fat sheriff convincing himself.

Fred turned to Mike. "Worse than a batch of black flies. A man can't find no peace with that."

"They'll go by Monday, Fred. Your liquor dope will work till then."

"Yeh, but it ain't right."

Mike watched the group. Several of them went directly to the pool table in the alcove adjacent to the main barroom. The others came up to the bar to order drinks and Harry went into motion. But one of them lingered behind. Her name was Allison Mills and Mike was watching her.

The girl stood back, behind those at the bar. She was dressed in faded blue jeans and a red check Malone shirt, open at the neck. Her black hair was cut short. She wore leather Indian moccasins which had colored beads over the toes. She was the most striking member of the group and she was standing back.

A young man in a blue blazer and plaid trousers handed Allison a dark-looking drink in a very tall glass. Then he moved off toward the pool table. She came over to Mike.

"Remember me?" she asked, taking the empty stool to his right and putting the tall glass on the bar.

"Sure," Mike said. "I haven't forgotten."

"You forgot to call, though. You said you'd call me. That was a year ago."

"I was never anywhere near you. I said I'd call if I came close."

"Oh, well," said Allison, raising the glass to her mouth

and moving her lips over the rim, "you could have called anyway." She licked the glass.

"What would I have done? Left a message that I called anyway?"

"Don't be ridiculous," Allison said. "I see you haven't changed."

"Meet Fred Monrovey," Mike said. The worker had not budged since playing the song.

"Hello," Allison said. "I hope you use a telephone better than Michael."

Fred just grinned and looked straight ahead at the whiskey bottles.

"So who are all these people?" Mike asked.

"Only people," said the girl.

The group had scattered. Some were at the pool table. Some were seated at tables in the main room. A few still stood at the bar. Wherever they were, they made noise.

"Why aren't all of you at the club?" Mike asked.

"Because we're here."

"I thought they were having a dance at the club."

"They are."

"You don't want to go?"

"Obviously. I may go later. I wanted to come here now."

"Sort of get dirty before you get clean."

"You said it," Allison said. "Not me. I'm leaving tomorrow. I'm only up for Labor Day."

"I don't think I've seen you this summer."

"You haven't. I was working in New York."

"Now you're going back to college?"

"I'm through with college," she said. "I graduated. Some of us still graduate."

"Well done," said Mike, and he ordered another beer for Fred and himself.

"I understand you taught tennis again," Allison said. "If I'd known that, I'd have come up for a lesson."

"We'd have accommodated you."

"I don't like lessons," the girl said. "They're so boring."

"It was nice of you not to come."

"Anyway I don't like the way you give them. How does it feel to spend the best years of your life showing rich kids how to whack a silly ball over a stupid net?"

"I teach them something," Mike said.

"I bet you do. I remember. How many lessons did you have to give that blonde waitress at the club before she learned?"

"She's not socially oriented. She doesn't play games."

"I could see that," said Allison.

"So you're staying at the club and secretly conducting an investigation of my activities?"

"I'm staying with Phillip," she said, indicating the fellow with the blue blazer. He was chalking a cue.

"Just because my parents are dumb enough to be members of the club doesn't mean I have to stay there. Or play tennis either."

"Nobody has to play," Mike said.

"What have you been doing besides playing with balls and waitresses?"

"I've been around."

"So I've heard," Allison said. She was smiling. She raised the tall glass and drained it completely, all but the ice. She set the glass on the bar with a thud.

"I'll buy you another," Mike said.

"Thanks. It's rum and Coke."

When he gave her a sour look, she said, "Do you mind? I like drinking rum and Coke in the summer. It's my drink."

Mike asked Harry to make her drink. Then he turned slightly toward her.

"Without school, what are you going to do when you leave here?"

"I want to do something."

"Get a job?"

"Yes."

"In New York?"

"Probably."

"You can make good money there."

"What's money?" she asked. "Everybody I know who has it doesn't know how to spend it."

"It's nice to have," Mike said, "And to spend."

"I don't know. Sometimes I think it's worthless. Phillip tells me I should do something worthwhile."

"Like what?"

"I don't know."

"What have you been doing?"

"Would you believe that for the last three months I've been working as a receptionist in practically the biggest bank in New York?"

Mike smiled.

"Yes," he said, "I would."

"Honestly it was so awful. I was really suffering. Everybody bothered me all the time about nothing. Finally I just had to quit. I don't know what I'll do now. I'm in no rush."

"You should be a cocktail waitress," Mike said, and he was rather pleased to have said it.

"You were waiting for that, weren't you? I'm sure you could teach me how. As I remember, you've got all the moves. Excellent service and all that."

"I don't think you'd make it to the top, kid."

"Thanks heaps," Allison said. She was starting on the second rum and Coke.

Now the bar was becoming packed. There were really

more locals then tourists or summer people but the locals were harder to see. They stood or sat at the bar, their shoulders hunched, talking quietly and drinking steadily. Or they sat at tables in corners. The others were more obvious.

Mike sipped his beer and tried to tally score. Allison was sitting next to him, he thought, because she wanted to. He had not done anything to encourage her. She had not even come to the bar with him. But she was certainly sitting with him now and her friend who was her host for the weekend was playing pool. Those were two solid points in his favor.

When Mike glanced at Allison, he thought she had more good looks than he had ever seen outside a magazine. And she was real and alive and close to him. That was another point. He did not mind her manner because he knew he could match her. The important point for him was that she had left her young man playing pool in his plaid pants and come over to sit with him. Mike figured he had nothing to lose by playing with her.

Fred was talking to Harry.

"I got to get out of here and go face the wife," he said.

Mike bought him another beer. Then he turned to Allison again.

"We were talking about what you were going to do."

"Right now, Mike, it's way up in the air."

"Where will it come down?"

"Phillip thinks I should go into modeling."

"What does this Phillip have to do with it?"

"Really nothing yet."

"What do you think you should do?"

"I already said I don't know. I'd like to try social work."

"I thought you'd ruled out being a barmaid."

"There you go," she said, laughing. "I'm trying to be serious."

"Be serious then."

"You know I get the feeling talking to you that you think I'm stupid."

"I get the feeling I've heard what you're saying before."

"You think I don't mean it?"

"No," said Mike seriously. "It isn't that. It's funny, but it seems like every time I get the chance to talk to you I've been doing a little drinking."

"You're drinking now," Allison said. "A little."

"That's what I mean but that's the point of this place."

"It's a nice place," she said, "And I'm drinking, too. So we're even."

She was smiling at him.

"You could be a model," he said.

"You don't think I'm too big here?" She put her hands on her chest.

"I never thought so. But maybe you should be a social worker."

They both started to laugh. They laughed until Fred leaned across Mike.

"You going to help out them coons, are you?" he asked.

Allison stopped laughing.

"Maybe," she said stiffly. "Maybe I'll just go to Europe."

"They ought to bomb all the niggers," Fred said. He was drunk now. He needed to keep his elbows on the bar for support. He held his head in his hands.

"The niggers ought to quit their goddamn bitching and go to work. I say give them a place of their own in the desert where they can start from nothing. Like they done with them Isreals, or whatever you call them. Them Jews. Then see how the coons do. Or else just bomb them."

"You must have given the problem alot of thought,"

Allison said. She was watching Mike, as if to learn how far she could go with Fred.

"Damn right I have," said Fred. "What it comes down to is it don't do no good to wash a skillet. Ain't that right, Harry?"

Harry would have replied but Fred dropped his arms on the bar and laid his head on top of them. Harry quickly moved the glass and beer bottle a safe distance away.

"He's had a few," Harry said.

"Swell friends you've got," said Allison. "Very interesting."

"He's all right. Just tired."

"I can see he's the type who makes things move along," she said. "Backwards."

"He works too hard."

"I bet he voted for Goldwater."

"Someday you might have to reach out and touch people like him. You know, you're an active social worker. He moves at his own pace, with his own problems."

"Just keep him out of any movement I'm in," said Allison. "I bet he's the type who won't ever change."

"He won't have to."

"But he will," she insisted. "That's the point."

"For whom?"

"We'll all have to. You will, too. I'm changing already."

"From socialite to social worker with a little modeling for Phillip sandwiched in between."

"That's not fair," she said. "I'm trying to be serious. And coming from the backcourt, that's almost a laugh."

"Deuce," said Mike. "I'm sorry."

"I mean it," Allison went on. "There has to be change. Today you've got a system where the government spends its time and money promoting a vicious, immoral war and protecting untold poverty and suffering. It prevents honest revolutionary change and it does it all in the name of peace. It's repressive and corrupt."

"I thought you'd finished your college," Mike said. "You sound like that William Sloane Coffin."

"Just let me finish. You've also got your friends like Fred there who blindly support this system. They can't even get the education to know they're getting the worst end of it."

"Start with him then. Wake him up and tell him what you've told me. You know what his response will be?"

"What?" asked Allison, leaning closer to him.

"First he'll tell you to shut your mouth. Then he'll tell you he works for a living but that, if you have any money or anything else besides theories you want to give away, he'll take it. Then he'll tell you to mind your own business."

"Then he's hopeless."

"He'll have been watching your crotch the whole time."

Mike leaned back with his hands on the bar. He felt the advantage was his.

"Then he's an ass," Allison said.

"He's an honest ass."

"He's drunk."

"He's a drunk honest ass."

"He's still an ass."

"You're not going to change him."

"I'm not going to try."

"What about all the others like him?"

"Enough of them will change. They'll see."

"We'll see."

"What about you?"

"You said it yourself. I whack little white balls over nets. I do it for money."

"And chase the skirts of cocktail waitresses at racist, establishment country clubs."

"That too, sometimes. It's all in a day's work."

"You're the worst," she said. "You're worse than what's his name there."

"His name's Fred. But hold it. Most of the time I'm back along the baselines coaching both sides."

"That's exactly what I mean. You don't get involved."

"It's better than just keeping score."

"Who does that? I intend to do more."

"Well do it then."

"I will."

"Give me a call when you do. I'll drop around and be a spectator."

"You do that," Allison said, raising her glass.

Then Mike felt a hand on his shoulder. When he turned, he was facing Allison's host.

"Well, how are we doing here?" asked the host, grabbing onto Mike's shoulder.

"This is Phillip Bourne," said Allison. "Phil, this is Mike Canby."

"Oh yes," said Phillip. "We've heard alot about you at the club, Mike." His voice rolled into the air like scented shaving cream. "Not all bad either, I might say. I understand you play some pretty mean croquet."

"He plays tennis," said Allison. "Don't be awful."

"Really? I used to play tennis once in awhile. Lately I've switched to golf. I find it a better game."

Bourne was keeping his hand on Mike's shoulder.

Mike examined him, seeing the obvious workshirt under the tailored blazer. The brass buckles on his highly polished shoes were as shiny as his face. His blonde hair looked corn yellow. When he had seen enough, Mike gave him his back.

"Phillip played tennis for Yale," Allison said with some pride.

"At Yale, Allie," Phillip corrected, "Not for Yale."

"Anyhow he's going to the University of North Carolina law school," she said.

"I think most of us are moving on to the club, Allie," said Phillip. "Things should be rolling. You'll probably want to change. Or are other matters pressing?"

Phillip chuckled softly. When finally he removed his hand from Mike's back, he swept it through his hair like a signal.

"Let's have one more drink here," said Allison.

"I don't know if I can stand it," Phillip said, but he rapped his glass on the bar until Harry came over.

"Cut out the noise," Harry said.

"Sorry, Harry," said Phillip, rising onto the balls of his feet to scan the rows of whiskey bottles. "Miss Mills, that's the lady here, will have another rum and Coke. Mike will have whatever he's drinking. Is it beer? Yes, it's beer. Give Mike a beer. I'll have whiskey and soda with no ice."

"What were you drinking?" asked Harry. "There's lots of whiskeys."

"Sorry again, Harry. If you remember correctly, I was drinking Scotch and I preferred Chevas Regal. You said you didn't have it so you switched me to Red Label."

"Don't make a goddamned case out of it," Harry said. "I'll give you whatever I got." He moved away to make the drinks.

"How'd the pool come out?" asked Allison.

"Rather well, actually. One more game and then we'll go. I hope I'm not interrupting anything. Was it tennis you teach?"

"Yes," said Mike, "It was."

"We should play sometime. Perhaps you could teach me a thing or two."

"I could try."

"I still play a few sets every now and then. Usually during the winter. When I'm in Florida."

"Mike's from Florida," said Allison.

"Really? We holiday in Boca Grande. The family's been going there for years. Don't you actually think golf is much more relaxing than tennis?"

"I actually wouldn't know," said Mike.

"I'd say this fellow looks pretty relaxed," Phillip said. He was pointing at Fred.

Fred was spread across the bar now but he opened an eye and asked, "Want me to move?"

"Lord no," said Phillip. "Don't try it."

"Stay there," Mike said. "You keep score."

"O.K., I'll keep score," said Fred, shutting the eye.

"I just haven't felt the need to join a golf club myself," Phillip said. "I'm sure I will eventually."

When Harry set the drinks in front of them, Phillip took his whiskey and drifted toward the pool table. Some of the group were trickling out the door to head for the club dance.

Mike said, "That Phillip looks good enough to package and sell."

"He's harmless and he's very nice," Allison said. "His parents have a gorgeous camp."

"I bet he touches up his hair every night and waxes his face with cold cream."

Allison did not touch her fresh drink. She put her right arm on the bar and leaned toward Mike.

"You sound jealous," she said. "That's supposed to be a sin."

"It's a hell of a fine night outside," Mike said. "The old moon is especially sinful."

"I didn't notice."

"It is anyway."

"Is that right?" asked Allison. She kept her eyes on his. Her lips were tight together and she was staring at him. He thought she looked foreign.

After awhile without speaking, she said, "Scientists always have such big buildings to work in. You'd think they'd be bigger men. Like basketball players."

"They've got big ideas," Mike said, speaking slowly and admiring her eyes. He was staring right back at her without really hearing what he was saying.

"It's hard enough to work with the ideas," he said. "They don't have to match them physically."

"It would be nice though," she said. She inched her hand along the bar until it was at his arm. Then it was climbing his shoulder. He was leaning in toward her.

"When will you be leaving?" she asked softly.

"I may not. I'm getting to like this very much."

"I have to leave tomorrow."

"That's not until tomorrow."

"It must get very dull for you around here when everyone's gone."

"It doesn't have to," Mike said. He took her hand off his shoulder and held it.

"When will you leave?" she asked again, her voice faintly hoarse.

"It might take the snow to push me out."

"Where will you go?"

"Back to Florida."

"Not to New York?"

"No."

"I think you're a lucky bum."

"I think I need the money. I can always find work in Tampa if I read the classified."

"Will you call me this time when you come through New York?"

"This time I think I'll fly direct from Montreal."

Then, abruptly, Mike was laughing at her and feeling just as pleased as if he had won an important set with an ace serve.

Allison jerked her hand out of his and jumped off the stool.

"You're still a goddamn rat," she said.

"I know," Mike said, laughing harder. "But it was good fun both times. Very relaxing and all that."

He watched her strut toward Phillip. She grabbed the gentleman by his shoulder and dragged him toward the door.

Mike spun around and shook Fred.

"I'm sorry. I lost track," Fred said.

"Let's go home," Mike said. "I'll take you. You can come back for the truck in the morning."

"Where's the little girl?" Fred asked. He groaned and sat up. "The one that wants to be a communist or whatever the shit it is."

"She left. She had to go dancing."

"Oh, fuck that," said Fred. Then he rubbed his eyes and said, "Mike, old buddy, some you win. Some you just got to lose."

A MESS OF TROUBLE

Three empties stood on the bar. Two were John's. The third was Georgina's.

John had left in a huff and Freddie was out back doing something. Ben was drinking whiskey.

"I'll buy you a beer to keep you here," Georgina told Ben.

"Can't drink no beer," Ben said. "Where'd John go to?"

"He just went. He said he don't want to see me ever again. You heard that."

"He didn't mean it. He's still your husband, ain't he?"

"Come on. I'll buy you a beer. I want another, too."

"I told you I can't drink no beer. I already had four in town before I come here. None of them tasted good. The last two I didn't even want. This fellow bought the bar a drink. Do you know how long that bar is?"

Georgina nodded, as though she knew all the bars in inches.

"Long enough to make me glad it wasn't me that did the buying," Ben said. "That's how long it is."

"Then I guess I'll have to splurge," said Georgina. "I'll buy you whatever you're drinking."

"What for? Where's your husband at?"

"Who cares?" said Georgina.

"I don't," said Ben. "But where's Freddie?"

"'Turn your damn head. Here he comes."

"Now no beer," Ben said. "Where you been, man?"

"Out back," said Freddie.

"Washing or pissing?"

"Little of both, Ben."

"Real good. This lady wants to buy me a drink without her husband here."

"Your wife ain't here either," said Georgina.

"Is that all right, Freddie?" asked Ben.

"It's O.K. with me," said Freddie.

"He won't drink no beer," Georgina said.

"That right?"

"Get to work," said Ben.

Freddie measured the shot, holding the bottle at arm's length, as if he were scared of it. He dumped the whiskey into Ben's glass and got a fresh beer for Georgina. Then he took her money and made change.

"Here's to you, old lady," said Ben. He dipped the rim of his glass toward the woman before trying the drink.

"No, here's to you," said Georgina, drinking her beer from the bottle.

"I don't see how you do it. I can't take that stuff no more."

"You just said you had four in town. That's two more than I had all day."

"I had to go buy groceries," Ben said. "Prices is out of sight on everything."

"Restaurants are worse, dearie."

"I don't go out. There's no place to eat good around here. Might as well stay home."

"I'll stay home if the company's good," Georgina said. "Otherwise I'll go out. We went out tonight."

"When I go out," Ben said, "I like a steak that's not too big. About like this."

Ben put his thumbs and forefingers together tip to tip,

so they made a heart. Then he raised his hands to show Freddie who nodded.

"We both ate fish tonight," Georgina said.

"Yeh, sometimes that's good. But I like a steak with French fries and a mixed salad and coffee. Only thing I can't eat is gravy."

"John can live on gravy."

"Me too," Ben said. "I love gravy but I can't eat it. The other night my wife made chicken gravy and Jesus, I was sick. I took four Alka-Seltzers, one right after the other. Next morning I couldn't work till ten."

"You're sure it was the gravy?"

"Yeh, it's happened before. My guts gets to hurting something terrible and I start puking."

"Maybe you should see a doctor."

"I seen one last year. He said it was my gall bladder. Said he couldn't do nothing."

"That shouldn't bother your stomach. Maybe I should take care of you."

"It gets me in my chest and back. My kidneys, too. I'm loose anyway. I go to the bathroom four or five times a day. I'm there soon as my feet hit the floor in the morning."

"Oh," said Georgina, and now she was looking at Freddie.

"Onions are what gets me," said Freddie.

"Yeh, Jesus," Ben said. "Don't them onions make you fart?"

"Sure do," said Freddie, smiling.

"Ben," said Georgina and she put her hand on his arm.

"I used to eat onions just like apples," Ben said, ignoring her hand. "The worst is when you get in bed and it's cold. Them onions just keep sneaking out. Matter of fact, I had an onion tonight."

Georgina dropped her hand.

"I'm leaving," she said.

"Where you going? You didn't finish your beer yet."

"I can't drink any more beer," Georgina said.

"But where you going?"

"I'm going to find John."

"Go," said Ben. "He probably needs finding by now."

When she had left, Ben told Freddie, "You know, I can eat almost anything. I don't care for caviar or nothing fancy like that, but there's damn few things I won't eat. What I love best is gravy. I like to eat it with bread."

Freddie nodded. He was grinning when he picked up the three empty bottles and the one half full.

TRACKS IN THE SNOW

Outside fine snow fell on Franz Ludwig's farmhouse. A sporadic wind from Canada drifted the new snow against the low building. When the wind subsided, the snowy Adirondack valley had a stillness that could be tasted. The valley was dark and very cold.

Before nightfall when the day had been grayest, the radio station in Plattsburgh referred to the storm as a blizzard. In the valley this meant the upstate roads would be closed at least to Albany and nobody at the radio station dared to predict when they would reopen. A blizzard was nothing new to the valley. It was certainly not an inconvenience.

Now the snow was quiet as it gathered and drifted. Even the hesitant wind from the border made little noise.

Inside the Ludwig farmhouse the air was close and cheerful, warmed by woodfires and conversation.

"Sam, take another piece of pie to the sitting room," Edith Ludwig told her guest. "Go ahead now. Franz, you show Sam the way. I'll bring fresh coffee."

Five of them were seated at the painted kitchen table. They had finished a large meal and all of them had eaten too much. An enormous amount of used blue dishes was stacked on the counter. On the table were open canner's jars of apple butter, corn relish, and shiny watermelon pickles. There was also a crusty tin of dark strawberry preserves and an empty gravy boat that did not match the other china. It had not been removed for dessert. Most of these foodstuffs were homemade, put up in the fall.

Sam Abernathy watched the two Ludwig children. They were eyeing the last piece of their mother's pie.

"I shouldn't," he said. "I had two pieces."

Sam looked at the children and then over at the white carcass near the sink. Clean ribs were all that remained of Edith's roast, hardly enough for soup. He figured he had eaten a third of the roast. Nothing was left of the meal except a few biscuits and the one wedge of pie.

"I really shouldn't," Sam said.

"Why in hell not?" asked Franz.

"Circumstances."

"Why don't you take that piece of pie and put it in your mouth," the little girl said, "then swallow."

"I guess I'll do that," said Sam, laughing at her. And he did take the pie, dousing it heavily with rough cinnamon.

The men rose first from the table. They took their time getting up and then going to the sitting room. They left Edith with the two children to clear the table.

Compared with the kitchen, the other rooms of the house were poorly lighted and always vaguely musty. This mustiness was expected. It lived from room to room in all seasons, like an ordinary housecat. Now the rich scents of the meal mingled with the smell of burning yellow birch. The combination of odors was pleasant and easy to get used to because, like the snow outside, it seemed to belong.

As the men changed rooms, Sam held the plate and thought about this most familiar smell of burning hardwood and how good it was all the time. He thought it was better than wildflowers and as good as the fragrance of women in his youth. Then he caught himself thinking and he realized he did not often catch himself thinking that way anymore. He blamed the meal and the two real whiskeys he had shared with Franz before dinner. Certainly he was not tired yet.

Then, still changing rooms slowly, Sam thought about how he could remember certain smells long after they were gone and how he was glad to have known certain of them at least once. Then he was in the sitting room and he stopped thinking and he laughed out loud at his thoughts and at the smells which had triggered his mind along with the whiskey.

"I got a nose like a damn bear," he said.

"Almost as big," said Franz. "You want a shot?"

"I think I better be happy the way I am."

"You look happy."

"Maybe I should have been some kind of poet," Sam said, laughing.

"Then you wouldn't have been happy. You'd have starved. All poets starve."

"As if you knew poets, Franz."

"I knew a poem once. Can't say I've met any real poets, though. Not the kind with the butterfly nets. Maybe they're hard to run down. But I'll tell you one thing, Sam. I bet they're mostly dull when you catch them."

The men laughed at this nonsense. They were both feeling traces of the whiskey.

"Well, so do farmers starve," Sam said. "Leastways the ones I know do."

"Ain't that the truth," Franz said, "But you sure can't eat words."

Franz was working a toothpick with his lips.

Sam's dog Stella lay by the hearth. She looked more like a bunched up throwrug than a border collie and she did not move when the men entered the room. She was the only dog in the house.

Sam walked to the hearth and peered down at her. She was aging now but she seemed very content by the fire. She only wanted to be left alone and to be comfortable.

"Fine meal, Franz," Sam said, and he adjusted his spectacles which were fogged faintly from the heat.

Franz nodded. "The wife can cook. That's why I married her."

He reached under his sweater to loosen his belt a notch before collapsing into the sunken armchair that was always his seat when he was in the room. They heard some of the old snow crash off the roof. Then Franz was seated and trying to be comfortable in the easy chair. Except for the fire, the room was quiet.

Sam stood at the fireplace and ate the last piece of pie off the mantle. He was a large, solid man with big bones. His coarse hair was almost white, parted neatly to reveal a line of pink scalp. His face was as tough as his cracked leather boots. His clothing was heavy and rough.

"Late for a real snow," Franz said, looking smaller than he was in the big chair.

"Just late weather," Sam said. "Except it was holding when I came over. Usually if a fellow don't like it this time of year, he can stick around five minutes and it'll change."

"You'll have to do better than that, poet," Franz said. "Seems like I've heard that one more than a few times before. True enough though."

Franz was breathing deeply, as if to catch up with himself after the meal. The chair seemed to have swallowed him.

Sam said, "Been something of a poor winter. I make it seven trouble snows before this little surprise. There's a lot on the ground."

Franz grunted from deep in the chair. "I didn't hear any late news. It was supposed to stop before now. News is all bad these days."

"It sure is," said Sam, bending over to eat the pie.

Franz said, "Might as well not pay no attention is what I say. I won't start to listen until baseball begins. I bet the main roads are closed from here to Saratoga though. We should have elected Goldwater when we had the chance."

"We should care," said Sam.

Franz laughed. He looked too comfortable to care about anything now.

"Yep, we should care about nothing. I guess no church tomorrow. Maybe the kids can ski after chores. They were getting ready for fishing."

"Me too," said Sam.

"Me too, but I like to see them ski."

"Planting's going to be late." Sam said, as if it mattered. His mouth was full.

When Edith appeared with the coffee, Sam left the fireplace to sit by her. They sat down together on the only sofa. It had been yellow once but it was now tan. Like the chair, the sofa was sunken.

Edith filled the three brown mugs carefully. Steam rose at the ceiling. She set down the pot and took up her sewing.

Sam said, "Fine dinner, Edie. The best in the valley I always say."

"You should come more often, Sam," the woman said. "You don't have to wait for an invitation. There's always enough for you. If there's not, we'll make more."

Sam watched her sew. He greatly admired the woman. He could tell she was tired from the long winter indoors but he knew she would not complain. Her face was always full but now it seemed tight, holding no anticipation. He looked at her hands. When Edith sewed, she squinted, using her fingers to search with the needle, as if probing for a bug living in the material. Sam decided she should buy glasses for her sewing, as he watched her hands.

With the dishes washed and stacked, the children came into the living room. They each had ice creams and they held the cones cautiously at arms length. In the weak light of the room they appeared like twins.

Sam tried to distinguish who was the girl. He knew she was two years younger but she was the same size as her brother. Their mother had cut her hair to the same boy's length and she wore the same rough shirts and trousers as her brother. Although they were both young, the girl was still very much a girl.

The children did not resemble anyone else in the room, Sam thought. They were fine children who could carry their own weight. Probably they already had, many times. Still they were untarnished and so different from their parents. Remembering how they had been mostly silent during the meal, Sam wondered briefly about the secrets they shared only with themselves, perhaps while skiing on those warm early spring afternoons when the world itself was growing. Briefly Sam regretted both the late storm's intrusion and the fact that he did not know either of these children well.

The girl brought her ice cream across to the fireplace and knelt to touch Stella. When the dog did not move, she returned to her brother. Then the children said goodnight like a pair of choirboys, scared but well rehearsed at their first mass, and they vanished into the room that had the Motorola television set.

"They're special kids," Sam said, after they had shut the door.

"They sure don't say much, do they?" Franz asked.

"No, they just tell you how to eat."

Edith looked up. Avoiding her husband, she said, "They're both young yet. They'd like to own a dog. They're old enough for that."

"A waste," Franz said immediately. "They know they'll not be having any dog. What does a dirt farmer want with a dog?"

"Wruff, dear," said Edith. "Company."

"I don't need no dogs for company."

"I wasn't talking about you," said Edith smiling. She

knew the children could have a dog if they shoved their
father gently. But she knew they would not push him. Franz
was tight with his earnings until he dared to be generous.
Then he was more than generous. His family was never
lacking.

"I might get them a horse if they learn to work him,"
Franz said. "They're tender yet, but horses are better than
dogs as pets. They don't lie around all day and they don't
run wild and chase deer at night. They don't waste
everybody's time."

"Is Stella a waste, Sam?" asked Edith, working the
needle without jabbing.

"Now what's he supposed to answer to that, Mother?"
Franz asked.

Sam fingered his shirt collar and then he rubbed his big
red hands on his knees. His hands were leathery, like his
face.

"Hard to say, Edie. The dog's about all I got. I suppose
she earns her keep by being that. She don't eat much
anymore."

"She's company, Sam." Edith said.

More snow crashed off the roof, landing with a thud.
Sam rose and walked to the window. The panes were frosty
at top and bottom.

"I believe it's quitting," he said. "Now we'll take a
westerly and plenty of warm rain, thank you." Again he was
thinking of planting.

"It'll stay cold," Franz said, and he emerged from the
large chair by sitting straight up. "Tell me, poet, can you
find a difference between green checks and green grass? I
sure as hell can't. This snow can keep on forever as far as
I'm concerned. So long as those checks don't stop."

The fire hissed. Its flames rose, meeting no resistance.
In the quick bright light Sam saw the razor nicks on the
younger man's face. He had noticed them at dinner and he

had tried not to stare but he was watching them now as he returned to stand by the hearth.

Sam stood with his back to the fire so the flames seemed to be lapping at his boots. His head was hidden in the darkness above the mantle but the rest of him made a tall silhouette. He was looking down and out at Franz when he said slowly, "I endorse all mine and send them over to folks that need them. I don't want no charity."

Sam turned to fill his pipe from the Prince Albert tin that was a permanent fixture on the Ludwig's mantle.

"You don't either," said Edith, without interrupting her sewing.

"If you'd have asked, Edie, you'd have found I do. I always have. Ever since they started coming."

"Then you're the only person in the whole damn valley who does," Franz said loudly. "Probably in the country at that."

"I could be the only one who does a lot of things," Sam said.

Franz drew out his own pipe and pointed the chewed black bit at Stella. Because of the light, his finger seemed to be extended. His hand was steady but pale, like a long spur of sand uncovered at low tide.

Pointing with the pipe, Franz said, "Except for this hound, Sam, you've nothing to worry about. Nothing at all. We happen to be a family."

"I never had a family," Sam said. "You know that."

"Let me finish. With the kids, we need the checks. We ain't ashamed to admit it. I'll have you know the checks do help some people."

When Franz brought down the pipe and relaxed, his face was flushed.

Sam was smoking.

"No offense," he said, "but to set the record straight for me. Not you. Just me. And then to drop it. I have never

cashed a single one of them checks for myself. Even when I
might have used them. And I don't intend to start now.
They take more out of you than they give back. And I ain't
never been to Washington, or to Albany more than I had to,
or to wherever it is that they write them up. What's more, I
don't never want to go. Now that's for me, Franz. That's my
way. I'm getting too old for nonsense."

Edith had been spinning quick circles around a newly
placed button. She snapped off the thread and said, "Most
arguments air better at the woodpile."

"It ain't no argument," said Franz. "It's just one man's
foolishness."

"Whatever it is," Edith said, "take it outside."

"It'll go by itself," said Sam.

Edith began another button. "Someday I'd like to take
the children down to Washington. A few of their school-
friends have gone already. They go this time of year."

"They go with the taxes," Franz said.

"I think children should see the monuments and where
the laws are made," Edith went on. She was speaking
casually, as if in a dream. And her voice was tender,
bordering on sadness, because she was mentioning things
her life did not permit. She did not notice her husband
thumb the Sears and Roebuck wishing book.

"Am I wrong to think that, Sam?" she asked.

"You're talking foolishness just like him," Franz said.

Sam shifted his weight before the fire.

"I don't know if you're wrong, Edie, but I'm old
enough to know that the important laws, them that I got to
live by, are made right here in this valley. I ain't speaking
for your town committee, or whatever those elected dudes
are calling themselves these days. I'm speaking for myself.
For me important laws are made by how a wind blows and
when that first warm rain finally gets here and melts this
damn snow. I follow easy laws like that. Like whether the

old sun is right at the right time. Those are laws I need to study. Those say about Franz's apples and his spuds and about how high my sweet corn will stretch. Those are my only laws and my monuments, too. And an old man like me can't even help to make them. He just lives by them like he always has, and he gets along. At least I think so."

When Sam finished his speech, he felt ridiculous. He said, "Forgive me. I talk too much. I always have. Most times there's nobody to listen. I better shut up now. Sorry to sound like a fool preacher."

Franz laughed and said, "You really spoke your peace, preacher, but that pie you just ate was probably paid for by the government. You seemed to like at least three slices of it."

"Yep, that's right," said Sam. "But I didn't need it. I did like it though. Good pie, Edie."

"You'd take to the checks if you were starving, or your family needed boots."

"I wouldn't have to be starving, Franz, so long as I could get around."

"You can never tell, Sam," said Edith. "Your laws can run slim. They can turn on you."

Franz struck a match to relight his pipe. "You pay your taxes, don't you? Or don't them kind of laws affect you neither?"

The younger man let the question linger in the air. He puffed on his pipe until he had won a slight nod from his guest.

Then he said, "You damn well deserve whatever they're willing to give you back. It was yours to start. That's the way I look at it. That's nothing but common sense."

Sam was fidgeting by the fire. He looked around the room. He knew a dimestore picture of Venice hung above the sofa. It hung at a slight angle to the floor and was never straightened. The picture was difficult to see at night. Sam looked for it now.

Gradually he saw the cheap wooden frame, and he was thinking how yellow the city of Venice somewhere in Italy always looked by day in the Ludwig's home and how black it was at night. Sam knew nothing about Venice except, from this picture, that the streets were water there without snow, and the cars boats, and that everything there could be yellow like the Ludwig's sofa used to be.

Sam did not answer Franz until he had found the picture. By then he had switched his gaze to the window with its fine overlay of crystal frost, finer even than the reproduction, and more normal. And Sam was thinking he could outlast any winter in the valley, no matter how poor, on the profits from his crops and on his own skill. He thought he had the right to disregard the government checks, and to consider them as loss rather than profit. He was wise to keep no livestock. With only himself, the dog, and the old John Deere to feed, he could manage. The tractor had the most expensive tastes. It ate gas.

But Sam knew it was different when you had a family. So he said, "It ain't easy, Franz. Sometimes it's hard. It's just I never did like the idea of sending what I earned down to Albany or Washington and having them take the prime cuts and then turn around and send me back nothing but stew meat."

He leaned over and knocked his pipe against the andiron to free the dead ash. Pipesmoke dominated the room. It was like the inside of a trapper's cabin, dark and close, except Edith was there.

"You can't change things, Sam," the woman said. "You might as well keep your checks and put them to use."

"I sure wish they'd never started that business. They were the bad weed in Roosevelt's patch. He was supposed to be a New Yorker."

Edith chuckled. "But they have started, Sam, quite a while back. You better climb aboard."

"Too late, Edie."

"Too contrary, you mean," said Franz.

"No, it's not, Sam," Edith said, and she stopped chuckling.

Sam looked at his dog. "You want to switch onto charity, old gal, or are you content with the way we've been handling things so far?"

He did not feel foolish for questioning the dog.

"Goddammit, it ain't charity," said Franz.

Stella opened one eye. She knocked her long tail against the floor. They were watching the dog closely as though they expected an answer.

When she shut the eye, Sam said, "Seems she don't like the idea. She don't want to look at it. I think we'll just leave things as they are."

"Then she's stupid," said Franz. "And, by God, you're stupider. You're just a fool who's listened to a dog for too damn long."

"But, Franz, she don't complain. Neither do I. She's all I got to keep from complaining. She don't need new boots. She don't eat into profits. And she don't demand no handouts. I reckon I'll go along with her."

"Go ahead. Be a fool."

"It's nice to understand her, Sam," Edith said. She was chuckling.

Franz jerked himself up to inspect the coffeepot.

"Then that's settled," he said. "You are one stubborn man, Sam Abernathy. You've lived alone and listened to a dog for too long. You must be blind to what's happened in this country."

"I can see good," Sam said, "if I can find my spectacles."

"You are worse than any politician," Franz told him. He saw the pot was dry and he slammed the lid shut.

"I'll get more," Edith said. "It's ready."

"You will not get more," her husband said. "You'll just stay put right where you are and try to make a little bit of sense with this man. I will get the coffee."

Edith could not help laughing at Franz. When he had left the room with the pot, she said, "He thinks he's right and he is right that those checks help us."

Sam came over and sat next to her.

"For you he's right, Edie. I can do without."

"You think they humble you?"

"I never found out," said Sam.

Again he watched her sew under the yellow painting of Venice which was hard to see at night. Her stubby fingers moved quickly over a patch she was sewing onto a pair of child's denim trousers. The clothes she had repaired while the men talked were stacked neatly between her and Sam.

These clothes are winter hay, Sam thought. I've seen them before. And Edith is like the foreign farming women on the cardboard prints that used to hang in the Saranac Lake Hotel. Those pictures were wheat colored, sort of dirty yellow, dirtier than Venice, not clean like snow. But it's true those women were hearty. They were not living on charity. The clothes are winter hay, Sam thought. Where am I thinking? Am I so old that I can think this way without making sense? He realized he was staring at the woman.

"Tomorrow's Sunday, Sam," Edith said. "Will you go to church with us?"

"Wedding or funeral?" Sam said, making a joke of it.

"Just services," said Edith.

Sam's eyes caught the crucifix. The crude plastic figure hung over the extra woodpile where he had hung his coat. It was nearly concealed. Sam was thinking that, regardless of what Franz had said earlier, the Ludwig family would go to church tomorrow. Even if they had to crawl through the snowdrifts. Sam always felt the urge to tear crucifixes from walls. He considered them a great obscenity.

"I'm supposed to be a damn poor Methodist," he said. "I've been one for years. I'd better not go anywhere but home."

"For a poor man, Sam, you have a wealth of excuses. You should go to services. You really should. It would be good for you."

"I've loaned my space permanently to a regular, Edie. I always liked the preacher who told his Christmas gathering he'd see them again on Easter. I reckon they'll be full enough tomorrow. I have lots of real work that needs doing before the ice goes out."

Sam fidgeted again.

Edith stopped and said, "Sit with us, Sam. There's room. The snow will keep some away."

Franz brought the coffee. He seemed pleased to have managed it alone. He was smiling when he stopped to fill the mugs.

"You get our poet untracked?" he asked.

"Still stuck to the hubs," Sam said. "We're off the checks and onto churches."

"Edith, you know that's not fair," Franz said, sitting down.

"I never mind the prodding," Sam said, "But I'm kind of hard to get into the chute."

"It will be a nice service," Edith said, blowing on her mug.

Then Stella moaned and picked herself off the floor as if to scratch. But she just arched her neck and yawned at the ceiling. She snapped her jaws shut.

"Time to get along?" Sam asked. He knew they had already overstayed their welcome and he gulped his coffee hot. Striking another match for his pipe, he looked at the dying fire. He thought his own house would be cold.

"We should be saying goodnight now," he said. "As always, you've been neighborly."

Edith set aside her sewing and rose from the couch. "It was good to have you, Sam. Come across any time."

When Sam stood up, Stella went to the door. She waited as he took his Hudson Bay jacket off the peg near the crucifix. She watched him feel it thoroughly for wetness.

When Sam put on the heavy coat, he reached for his worn wallet, took out a five dollar bill, and gave it to Edith.

"What's this?" asked Franz.

"For the plate tomorrow. Charity for the church. Property of a poor Methodist and certainly not from the government."

"You don't let up, do you?" said Franz.

"I figure I owe them. I've ate a few chicken suppers there."

"Don't be ridiculous," said Franz.

"They'll still take your money, won't they?" Sam asked. He was grinning. He seemed enormous in the thick white jacket with the three broad candy stripes.

"They'll appreciate it," said Edith.

Franz swung open the front door and the sharp cold rushed against them. They saw the snow had stopped. The wind was working to settle it. The moon was full now and very bright on the carpet of fresh snow. For a long moment they were silent. It was as though all they saw and felt there in the farmhouse doorway made them each in his own way happy to be there and not to be anywhere else but in this valley. Then it was as though they had prayed.

They shook hands like neighbors and Sam put on his cap. He stepped out into the cold night where Stella was waiting.

"Take care of those kids," he said.

"You take care going home, poet," Franz said as he closed the door.

Sam's snowshoes stood heel under near the woodshed. In the moonlight they looked like two children hoping for a handout. They were pickerel shaped with slim treads, high upturns, and long tails for speed and balance.

Sam wanted to move quickly to keep the heat he had stored up in the house. But when he knocked the snow from the shoes, he dawdled to inspect them. With his bare hands, he felt the white ash frames and how they were battered, like a hockey stick becomes after hard play. He would have to revarnish the wood and store the shoes carefully if summer ever came. He poked at the cowhide webbings and decided the fine mesh at the toes and heels would last. But the coarser webbing of the bodies would need replacing before next season. The shoes were thirty years old. It had been a poor winter.

Another job, Sam thought, and at my age there are too many jobs just to keep going. He was annoyed both at the condition of the shoes and at himself.

As Sam knelt to buckle the binding straps across his boots, Stella barked. She was anxious to be home and warm again. The three minute spotcheck had taken too long. Sam stood up and put on his gloves.

Their path home led through the Ludwig's big apple orchard. With the full moon, Sam easily skirted the trees. The frail black lace branches were bending to their breaking point under the burden of more snow. Stella ducked the branches, running far ahead.

As Sam walked, he felt with his feet and kept his eyes on the dark line where the sky met the mountains. Fine crystal funnels of snow swirled around his legs and vanished in the wind. The fresh snow over the old base was light and very soft under his shoes. It was not yet a spring snow. Sam knew he could make good time and work off the dinner just by walking easily. He may have been old but he could still enjoy a long walk in the night.

With the moon full, the shadows were heavy in the orchard. Sam could even distinguish some of the pines on the mountains surrounding the valley quite close. The pines appeared and then moved away in the darkness, like a bunch of kneeling, well-starched nuns in winter habit, backing off from an altar.

Trees are noble, Sam thought. If I were really a poet, mostly I'd write about trees and how at night, if there is no moon, there are no trees. And how when there is no moon, there is nothing, and how when there is a moon, there is everything. Today there was this snow and there was also nothing. Tonight there is this moon. Although I can't write one word about it, it can be my moon and the snow is mine and the trees are my trees. I say they are noble trees.

When he was clear of the orchard and almost to the stone wall that marked the Ludwig's summer pasture, he heard Stella bark. He was working up a slight sweat in the heavy coat. He stopped to look back at the farmhouse. He saw a single light in the darkness.

Edith, he thought. She'll be setting the breakfast table or planning Sunday dinner. It will be a good dinner and I'll be eating beans. But that's my way.

Then, seeing the lone light in the distance and feeling the wind hard at his neck and the snow whirling at his feet, Sam could feel neither young nor old, only strangely alive.

Something different than this way I'm living now might have been, he told himself, but it's yours and you can't ever have regrets about anything. He spat in the snow and he set out again to catch the dog.

He reached the pasture wall where he had to sit down on a wet stone to swing his snowshoes across. He did not mind the slippery second of cold on the seat of his woolen trousers and he did not give it any attention with his hand. Now Sam was going strong.

When he righted himself and was in the pasture and had lost the farmhouse glow completely, he saw the tracks that had caused Stella to bark. They were very clean and fresh tracks, broken deep, apparently just before the dog had jumped the wall. In the moonlight Sam could see them clearly, like watermarks on blank white paper.

When he stopped and leaned over to examine the tracks, he saw how the deer was big and how, although the tracks were deep, he had been only lightly spooked by the dog. Then he saw how just three hooves had broken the snow exactly and how the fourth, the left front leg, had been dragged like a ski pole. Then Sam had recognized this deer.

"You old bugger," he said out loud. "What are you doing here this time of night?"

Sam removed his gloves, pulled out his pipe, and filled it. He had to cup his hands to light it. He did not feel the cold and he was smiling. For he knew the tracks below him, solid in the snow, and he knew the old buck, though only slightly spooked, would now be running fast ahead and paying no attention to his bad leg and stopping only when he decided to look back.

Somehow the oldtimer had kept his weight, Sam thought. And if this wasn't a poor winter, I'd sure like to see one.

Stella came out of the darkness and up to Sam's side. She was quivering at the chance of a chase.

"We don't want to run a buck like that," Sam said, ignoring the dog's eyes. "We'd be killing ourselves."

He had to relight his pipe and he struck another match.

"Or am I just too old?" he asked slowly, and he knew

he had lost the tight feeling that should have been in him hard like a fist at the first sight of the tracks.

"Which is it?" he asked, puffing to get the tobacco going. "If we were starving," he said. "If we could feel our ribs, then we'd give him a run. But we're both stuffed now."

Too old's the reason, he thought again, and he was growing chilled standing there in the windswept pasture with his dog trembling at his side. The valley was quiet all around.

"Age is something you only admit to yourself," he said.

There had been days, he thought, and there had been bad nights, when he was tired worse than this, when he would not have had any decision to make.

"Then I'd have had to follow," he told Stella. "I'd have had that feeling. It would have forced me. But now it's missing, girl. It's gone somewhere. Christ it was a good feeling when I had it. It almost carried its own smell. Now it's gone. There ain't nothing but an old man who's got no taste for a chase."

Sam stood in the snow, listening for nothing and hearing nothing, not even the wind. He was hating himself for his own emptiness and telling himself there was no point in following tracks without a rifle and that it was much better to leave this big buck alone.

"Let him come to us if he's tired of living," Sam said. "If he wants to take chances."

Yet the tracks led in his direction and he put on his gloves. Puffing his pipe, he struck out, his head bent into the wind.

The tracks that Sam now followed across the Ludwig's pasture were well known in the valley. They were almost as renown as Edith's cooking. Perhaps they were more respected.

Their fame was not limited to the valley. Each autumn

men would come from downstate, hoping especially to kill this buck. Once a hunter had nearly succeeded but maimed him instead. Then he had told about it and then more men had come, wearing their insulated rubber boots and the ill-fitting red clothing which was cumbersome and useless for every aspect of hunting except self-protection. They had all been disappointed. So they had also settled for telling tales of the buck's enormous size and how they had seen him or missed him or missed seeing him. By now there were too many tales about this deer and too many men who told them. Few were the men who had seen him outside their minds, or even his broken tracks.

Now Sam was following this deer's tracks across the pasture and he was thinking about the animal very much and about how men kept money pools in taverns over him and told their children about him again and again after all the other stories had gone stale.

Sam had hunted the valley as much as anyone but he had never had a crack at this deer or any other like him. Yet he knew him better than most of the redshirts. He knew the buck would range high in the endless meandering pine ridges during the hunting season. He would stay above the valley. He would stay on the move, using each of those too many places which made men work when they tried to reach them, and then made them shiver when they sat down to wait with only their luck and a cheese sandwich for comfort. He would conceal himself all day on the ridges where he could scout the gulches and the valley floor. At night he would come down to feed on beechnuts, to drink in the many streams. He would stick to his irregular pattern and remain hidden until all the hunters had gone home with a fresh Christmas tree or a miserable hot doe souring across their automobile hoods. Then he would begin to buy his winter outfit.

Gradually snow would force him lower and his coat

would have turned blue when he came and he would have collected and abandoned his harem and still he would not be gaunt. He would begin to live in the low timber apart from his does. By day he would rest, soaking up sun. By night he would forage, sometimes scraping apple orchards, like Franz Ludwig's, where early snow preserved late fruit until early rain came to rot it finally.

Now, Sam thought, when he is spoiled by his freedom and has no fear and when his food is still scarce, now would be the best time to kill this fellow.

Sam shook off the cold and then he was imagining he could hear the deer running ahead. He began to feel his closeness but the feeling would not be important unless he could smell it. He thought about collecting his rifle. He would have good tracking until dawn and then the buck would rest, thinking himself safe. With luck on the wind, getting close in the snow would be easy.

"I've done it enough," Sam said softly. "Damned if I haven't. And I've done it plenty out of season. When the belly won't quit grumbling, you track them any way they come. I could do it again. But I won't. Now I track myself to the IGA store."

I'm just too old, Sam thought. Too damn comfortable. Now I'm stuffed to boot.

Sam increased his pace on the worn snowshoes. The buck would be far out ahead and sure of himself now.

"He's got to be pretty special to have stuck it out with that bad leg," Sam said. "He sure can't hide it. It's like the old age. It's like that last silly wager nobody beats. It's like when the mountain frowns on you. You just accept that and you make do."

Sam shivered under the heavy coat. His pipe was cold and he put it away.

He ain't got no head worth anything now noway, Sam thought.

"Go on, you bastard. If ever I'd have been a poet, I'd have made a pretty foolish one."

When he reached the birch grove which marked his own property, Sam stopped. He shook his head as if to clear it. He saw his own land. He thought his land looked the way a farmer's land in winter was supposed to look. It was flat and quiet, as though only a wise old deer with a bad leg would ever use it for anything.

When he left the tracks to take the shortcut home where Stella would be waiting, Sam was laughing softly. His laughter hung in the cold night air, seeming to last, like children pressuring the town drunk.

He moved slowly. He was remembering both parts of the evening. Then he was thinking about how difficult it was becoming to find decent hardwood among all the soft pines. And then about how difficult hardwood could be to cut once it had been found. Then, with the moon overflowing behind him, Sam reminded himself that any hardwood was worth the effort when stacked neatly by the barn against a late winter's storm.